THE MICHIGAN HISTORICAL REPRINT SERIES

*Reprints from the collection of
the University of Michigan
University Library*

This volume is produced from digital images created through the University of Michigan University Library's preservation reformatting program. The Library seeks to preserve the intellectual content of items in a manner that facilitates and promotes a variety of uses. The digital reformatting process results in an electronic version of the text that can both be accessed online and used to create new print copies. This book and thousands of others can be found in the digital collections of the University of Michigan Library. The University Library also understands and values the utility of print, and makes reprints available through its Scholarly Publishing Office.

For access to the University of Michigan Library's digital collections, please see http://www.lib.umich.edu.

The Scholarly Publishing Office seeks to disseminate high-quality, cost-effective scholarly content through both print and electronic publishing. Information about the Scholarly Publishing Office can be found at http://spo.umdl.umich.edu.

THE SCHOLARLY PUBLISHING OFFICE
THE UNIVERSITY OF MICHIGAN
UNIVERSITY LIBRARY

Modern Classics.

MY GARDEN ACQUAINTANCE,
A GOOD WORD FOR WINTER,
A MOOSEHEAD JOURNAL.
By JAMES RUSSELL LOWELL.

THE FARMER'S BOY.
By ROBERT BLOOMFIELD.

ILLUSTRATED.

BOSTON:
HOUGHTON, MIFFLIN AND COMPANY.
The Riverside Press, Cambridge.

MY GARDEN ACQUAINTANCE

AND

A GOOD WORD FOR WINTER.

CONTENTS.

MY GARDEN ACQUAINTANCE.

NE of the most delightful books in my father's library was White's Natural History of Selborne. For me it has rather gained in charm with years. I used to read it without knowing the secret of the pleasure I found in it, but as I grow older I begin to detect some of the simple expedients of this natural magic. Open the book where you will, it takes you out of doors. In our broiling July weather one can walk out with this genially garrulous Fellow of Oriel and find refreshment instead of fatigue. You have no trouble in keeping abreast of him as he ambles along on his hobby-horse, now pointing to a pretty view, now stopping to watch the motions of a bird

or an insect, or to bag a specimen for the
Honorable Daines Barrington or Mr. Pen-
nant. In simplicity of taste and natural
refinement he reminds one of Walton ; in
tenderness toward what he would have called
the brute creation, of Cowper. I do not
know whether his descriptions of scenery are
good or not, but they have made me familiar
with his neighborhood. Since I first read
him, I have walked over some of his favorite haunts, but I still see them through his
eyes rather than by any recollection of actual
and personal vision. The book has also the
delightfulness of absolute leisure. Mr. White
seems never to have had any harder work to
do than to study the habits of his feathered
fellow-townsfolk, or to watch the ripening
of his peaches on the wall. His volumes
are the journal of Adam in Paradise,

> " Annihilating all that 's made
>   To a green thought in a green shade."

It is positive rest only to look into that garden of his. It is vastly better than to

> " See great Diocletian walk
> In the Salonian garden's noble shade,"

for thither ambassadors intrude to bring with them the noises of Rome, while here the world has no entrance. No rumor of the revolt of the American Colonies seems to have reached him. "The natural term of an hog's life" has more interest for him than that of an empire. Burgoyne may surrender and welcome ; of what consequence is *that* compared with the fact that we can explain the odd tumbling of rooks in the air by their turning over " to scratch themselves with one claw" ? All the couriers in Europe spurring rowel-deep make no stir in Mr. White's little Chartreuse ; but the arrival of the house-martin a day earlier or later than last year is a piece of news worth sending express to all his correspondents.

Another secret charm of this book is its inadvertent humor, so much the more delicious because unsuspected by the author. How pleasant is his innocent vanity in adding to the list of the British, and still more of the Selbornian, *fauna !* I believe he would gladly have consented to be eaten by a tiger or a crocodile, if by that means the occasional

presence within the parish limits of either
of these anthropophagous brutes could have
been established. He brags of no fine society, but is plainly a little elated by "having considerable acquaintance with a tame
brown owl." Most of us have known our
share of owls, but few can boast of intimacy
with a feathered one. The great events of
Mr. White's life, too, have that dispropor-
tionate importance which is always humor-
ous. To think of his hands having actually
been thought worthy (as neither Willough-
by's nor Ray's were) to hold a stilted plover,
the *Charadrius himantopus*, with no back toe,
and therefore "liable, in speculation, to perpetual vacillations"! I wonder, by the way,
if metaphysicians have no hind toes. In
1770 he makes the acquaintance in Sussex
of "an old family tortoise," which had then
veen domesticated for thirty years. It is
clear that he fell in love with it at first
sight. We have no means of tracing the
growth of his passion ; but in 1780 we find
him eloping with its object in a post-chaise.
"The rattle and hurry of the journey so per-

fectly roused it that, when I turned it out in a border, it walked twice down to the bottom of my garden." It reads like a Court Journal : " Yesterday morning H. R. H. the Princess Alice took an airing of half an hour on the terrace of Windsor Castle." This tortoise might have been a member of the Royal Society, if he could have condescended to so ignoble an ambition. It had but just been discovered that a surface inclined at a certain angle with the plane of the horizon took more of the sun's rays. The tortoise had always known this (though he unostentatiously made no parade of it), and used accordingly to tilt himself up against the garden-wall in the autumn. He seems to have been more of a philosopher than even Mr. White himself, caring for nothing but to get under a cabbage-leaf when it rained, or the sun was too hot, and to bury himself alive before frost, — a four-footed Diogenes, who carried his tub on his back.

There are moods in which this kind of history is infinitely refreshing. These creatures whom we affect to look down upon as

the drudges of instinct are members of a
commonwealth whose constitution rests on
immovable bases. Never any need of re-
construction there ! *They* never dream of
settling it by vote that eight hours are equal
to ten, or that one creature is as clever as
another and no more. *They* do not use their
poor wits in regulating God's clocks, nor
think they cannot go astray so long as they
carry their guide-board about with them, —
a delusion we often practise upon ourselves
with our high and mighty reason, that admirable finger-post which points every way
and always right. It is good for us now
and then to converse with a world like Mr.
White's, where Man is the least important
of animals. But one who, like me, has always lived in the country and always on the
same spot, is drawn to his book by other
occult sympathies. Do we not share his
indignation at that stupid Martin who had
graduated his thermometer no lower than 4°
above zero of Fahrenheit, so that in the coldest weather ever known the mercury basely
absconded into the bulb, and left us to see

the victory slip through our fingers just as
they were closing upon it ? No man, I suspect, ever lived long in the country without
being bitten by these meteorological ambi-
tions. He likes to be hotter and colder, to
have been more deeply snowed up, to have
more trees and larger blown down than his
neighbors. With us descendants of the Pu-
ritans especially, these weather-competitions
supply the abnegated excitement of the race-
course. Men learn to value thermometers
of the true imaginative temperament, capable of prodigious elations and corresponding dejections. The other day (5th July) I
marked 98° in the shade, my high-water
mark, higher by one degree than I had ever
seen it before. I happened to meet a neighbor ; as we mopped our brows at each other,
he told me that he had just cleared 100°,
and I went home a beaten man. I had not
felt the heat before, save as a beautiful exag-
geration of sunshine ; but now it oppressed
me with the prosaic vulgarity of an oven.
What had been poetic intensity became all
at once rhetorical hyperbole. I might sus-

pect his thermometer (as indeed I did, for we Harvard men are apt to think ill of any graduation but our own) ; but it was a poor consolation. The fact remained that his herald Mercury, standing a-tiptoe, could look down on mine. I seem to glimpse something of this familiar weakness in Mr. White. He, too, has shared in these mercurial triumphs and defeats. Nor do I doubt that he had a true country-gentleman's interest in the weathercock ; that his first question on coming down of a morning was, like Barabbas's,

'" Into what quarter peers my halcyon's bill ? "

It is an innocent and healthful employment of the mind, distracting one from too continual study of himself, and leading him to dwell rather upon the indigestions of the elements than his own. " Did the wind back round, or go about with the sun ? " is a rational question that bears not remotely on the making of hay and the prosperity of crops. I have little doubt that the regulated observation of the vane in many different places, and the interchange of results by telegraph, would put the weather, as it were, in our power, by betraying its ambushes before it is ready to give the assault. At first sight, nothing seems more drolly trivial than the lives of those whose single achievement is to record the wind and the temperature three times a day. Yet such men are doubtless sent into the world for this special end, and perhaps there is no kind of accurate observation, whatever its object, that has not its final use and value for some one or other. It is even to be hoped that the speculations of our newspaper editors and their myriad correspondents upon the signs of the political atmosphere may also fill their appointed place in a well-regulated universe, if it be only that of supplying so many more jack-o'-lanterns to the future historian. Nay, the observations on finance of an M. C. whose sole knowledge of the subject has been derived from a lifelong success in getting a living out of the public without paying any equivalent therefor, will perhaps be of interest hereafter to some explorer of our *cloaca maxima*, whenever it is cleansed.

For many years I have been in the habit
of noting down some of the leading events
of my embowered solitude, such as the coming of certain birds and the like, — a kind
of *mémoires pour servir*, after the fashion of
White, rather than properly digested natural
history.   I thought it not impossible that a
few simple stories of my winged acquaint-
ances might be found entertaining by per-
sons of kindred taste.

There is a common notion that animals
are better meteorologists than men, and I
have little doubt that in immediate weather-
wisdom they have the advantage of our so-
phisticated senses (though I suspect a sailor
or shepherd would be their match), but I
have seen nothing that leads me to believe
their minds capable of erecting the horoscope
of a whole season, and letting us know be-
forehand whether the winter will be severe
or the summer rainless.   I more than suspect that the clerk of the weather himself
does not always know very long in advance
whether he is to draw an order for hot or
cold, dry or moist, and the musquash is

scarce likely to be wiser. I have noted but
two days' difference in the coming of the
song-sparrow between a very early and a
very backward spring. This very year I
saw the linnets at work thatching, just before a snow-storm which covered the ground
several inches deep for a number of days.
They struck work and left us for a while,
no doubt in search of food. Birds frequently
perish from sudden changes in our whimsi-
cal spring weather of which they had no
foreboding. More than thirty years ago, a
cherry-tree, then in full bloom, near my
window, was covered with humming-birds
benumbed by a fall of mingled rain and
snow, which probably killed many of them.
It should seem that their coming was dated
by the height of the sun, which betrays them
into unthrifty matrimony ;

"So nature pricketh hem in their corages " ;

but their going is another matter. The
chimney-swallows leave us early, for example, apparently so soon as their latest fledglings are firm enough of wing to attempt the

long rowing-match that is before them.   On
the other hand, the wild-geese probably do
not leave the North till they are frozen out,
for I have heard their bugles sounding south-
ward so late as the middle of December.
What may be called local migrations are
doubtless dictated by the chances of food.
I have once been visited by large flights
of cross-bills ; and whenever the snow lies
long and deep on the ground, a flock of
cedar-birds comes in midwinter to eat the
berries on my hawthorns.   I have never
been quite able to fathom the local, or rather
geographical partialities of birds.   Never before this summer (1870) have the king-birds,
handsomest of fly-catchers, built in my orchard ; though I always know where to find
them within half a mile.   The rose-breasted
grosbeak has been a familiar bird in Brook-
line (three miles away), yet I never saw one
here till last July, when I found a female
busy among my raspberries and surprisingly
bold.   I hope she was *prospecting* with a view
to settlement in our garden.   She seemed,
on the whole, to think well of my fruit, and

I would gladly plant another bed if it would help to win over so delightful a neighbor.

The return of the robin is commonly announced by the newspapers, like that of eminent or notorious people to a watering-place, as the first authentic notification of spring. And such his appearance in the orchard and garden undoubtedly is. But, in spite of his name of migratory thrush, he stays with us all winter, and I have seen him when the thermometer marked 15° below zero of Fahrenheit, armed impregnably within, like Emerson's Titmouse, and as cheerful as he. The robin has a bad reputation among people who do not value themselves less for being fond of cherries. There is, I admit, a spice of vulgarity in him, and his song is rather of the Bloomfield sort, too largely ballasted with prose. His ethics are of the Poor Richard school, and the main chance which calls forth all his energy is altogether of the belly. He never has those fine intervals of lunacy into which his cousins, the catbird and the mavis, are apt to fall. But for a' that and twice as muckle 's a' that, I would not exchange him for all the cherries that ever came out of Asia Minor. With whatever faults, he has not wholly forfeited that superiority which belongs to the children of nature. He has a finer taste in fruit than could be distilled from many successive committees of the Horticultural Society, and he eats with a relishing gulp not inferior to Dr. Johnson's. He feels and freely exercises his right of eminent domain. His is the earliest mess of green peas; his all the mulberries I had fancied mine. But if he get also the lion's share of the raspberries, he is a great planter, and sows those wild ones in the woods, that solace the pedestrian and give a momentary calm even to the jaded victims of the White Hills. He keeps a strict eye over one's fruit, and knows to a shade of purple when your grapes have cooked long enough in the sun. During the severe drought a few years ago, the robins wholly vanished from my garden. I neither saw nor heard one for three weeks. Meanwhile a small foreign grape-vine, rather shy of bearing, seemed to find the dusty air

congenial, and, dreaming perhaps of its sweet
Argos across the sea, decked itself with a
score or so of fair bunches. I watched them
from day to day till they should have se-
creted sugar enough from the sunbeams, and
at last made up my mind that I would cele-
brate my vintage the next morning. But
the robins too had somehow kept note of
them. They must have sent out spies, as
did the Jews into the promised land, before
I was stirring. When I went with my basket, at least a dozen of these winged vin-
tagers bustled out from among the leaves,
and alighting on the nearest trees inter-
changed some shrill remarks about me of a
derogatory nature. They had fairly sacked
the vine. Not Wellington's veterans made
cleaner work of a Spanish town ; not Fed-
erals or Confederates were ever more impar-
tial in the confiscation of neutral chickens.
I was keeping my grapes a secret to surprise
the fair Fidele with, but the robins made
them a profounder secret to her than I had
meant. The tattered remnant of a single
bunch was all my harvest-home. How pal-

try it looked at the bottom of my basket, —
as if a humming-bird had laid her egg in an
eagle's nest! I could not help laughing;
and the robins seemed to join heartily in the
merriment. There was a native grape-vine
close by, blue with its less refined abundance, but my cunning thieves preferred the
foreign flavor. Could I tax them with want
of taste?

The robins are not good solo singers, but
their chorus, as, like primitive fire-worship-
pers, they hail the return of light and warmth
to the world, is unrivalled. There are a
hundred singing like one. They are noisy
enough then, and sing, as poets should, with
no afterthought. But when they come after
cherries to the tree near my window, they
muffle their voices, and their faint *pip, pip,
pop!* sounds far away at the bottom of the
garden, where they know I shall not suspect
them of robbing the great black-walnut of
its bitter-rinded store.* They are feathered

---

* The screech-owl, whose cry, despite his ill
name, is one of the sweetest sounds in nature,
softens his voice in the same way with the most
beguiling mockery of distance.

Pecksniffs, to be sure, but then how brightly
their breasts, that look rather shabby in the
sunlight, shine in a rainy day against the
dark green of the fringe-tree ! After they
have pinched and shaken all the life out
of an earthworm, as Italian cooks pound all
the spirit out of a steak, and then gulped
him, they stand up in honest self-confidence,
expand their red waistcoats with the virtu-
ous air of a lobby member, and outface you
with an eye that calmly challenges inquiry.
" Do *I* look like a bird that knows the flavor
of raw vermin ? I throw myself upon a jury
of my peers. Ask any robin if he ever ate
anything less ascetic than the frugal berry
of the juniper, and he will answer that his
vow forbids him." Can such an open bosom
cover such depravity ? Alas, yes ! I have
no doubt his breast was redder at that very
moment with the blood of my raspberries.
On the whole, he is a doubtful friend in the
garden. He makes his dessert of all kinds
of berries, and is not averse from early pears.
But when we remember how omnivorous he
is, eating his own weight in an incredibly

short time, and that Nature seems exhaustless in her invention of new insects hostile
to vegetation, perhaps we may reckon that he
does more good than harm.   For my own
part, I would rather have his cheerfulness
and kind neighborhood than many berries.

For his cousin, the catbird, I have a still
warmer regard.   Always a good singer, he
sometimes nearly equals the brown thrush,
and has the merit of keeping up his music
later in the evening than any bird of my
familiar acquaintance.   Ever since I can
remember, a pair of them have built in a
gigantic syringa, near our front door, and I
have known the male to sing almost un-
interruptedly during the evenings of early
summer till twilight duskened into dark.
They differ greatly in vocal talent, but all
have a delightful way of crooning over, and,
as it were, rehearsing their song in an undertone, which makes their nearness always
unobtrusive.   Though there is the most trust-
worthy witness to the imitative propensity
of this bird, I have only once, during an intimacy of more than forty years, heard him

indulge it. In that case, the imitation was by no means so close as to deceive, but a free reproduction of the notes of some other birds, especially of the oriole, as a kind of variation in his own song. The catbird is as shy as the robin is vulgarly familiar. Only when his nest or his fledglings are approached does he become noisy and almost aggressive. I have known him to station his young in a thick cornel-bush on the edge of the rasp-berry-bed, after the fruit began to ripen, and feed them there for a week or more. In such cases he shows none of that conscious guilt which makes the robin contemptible. On the contrary, he will maintain his post in the thicket, and sharply scold the intruder who ventures to steal *his* berries. After all, his claim is only for tithes, while the robin will bag your entire crop if he get a chance.

Dr. Watts's statement that "birds in their little nests agree," like too many others intended to form the infant mind, is very far from being true. On the contrary, the most peaceful relation of the different species to each other is that of armed neutrality. They are very jealous of neighbors. A few years ago, I was much interested in the house-building of a pair of summer yellow-birds. They had chosen a very pretty site near the top of a tall white lilac, within easy eye-shot of a chamber window. A very pleasant thing it was to see their little home growing with mutual help, to watch their industrious skill interrupted only by little flirts and snatches of endearment, frugally cut short by the common-sense of the tiny housewife. They had brought their work nearly to an end, and had already begun to line it with fern-down, the gathering of which demanded more distant journeys and longer absences. But, alas! the syringa, immemorial manor of the catbirds, was not more than twenty feet away, and these "giddy neighbors" had, as it appeared, been all along jealously watch-ful, though silent, witnesses of what they deemed an intrusion of squatters. No sooner were the pretty mates fairly gone for a new load of lining, than

"To their unguarded nest these weasel Scots
    Came stealing."

Silently they flew back and forth, each giving a vengeful dab at the nest in passing. They did not fall-to and deliberately destroy it, for they might have been caught at their mischief. As it was, whenever the yellow-birds came back, their enemies were hidden in their own sight-proof bush. Several times their unconscious victims repaired damages, but at length, after counsel taken together, they gave it up. Perhaps, like other unlettered folk, they came to the conclusion that the Devil was in it, and yielded to the invisible persecutions of witchcraft.

The robins, by constant attacks and annoyances, have succeeded in driving off the blue-jays who used to build in our pines, their gay colors and quaint noisy ways making them welcome and amusing neighbors. I once had the chance of doing a kindness to a household of them, which they received with very friendly condescension. I had had my eye for some time upon a nest, and was puzzled by a constant fluttering of what seemed full-grown wings in it whenever I drew nigh. At last I climbed the tree, in

spite of angry protests from the old birds
against my intrusion. The mystery had a
very simple solution. In building the nest,
a long piece of packthread had been somewhat loosely woven in. Three of the young
had contrived to entangle themselves in it,
and had become full-grown without being
able to launch themselves upon the air.
One was unharmed ; another had so tightly
twisted the cord about its shank that one
foot was curled up and seemed paralyzed ;
the third, in its struggles to escape, had
sawn through the flesh of the thigh and so
much harmed itself that I thought it hu-
mane to put an end to its misery. When I
took out my knife to cut their hempen bonds,
the heads of the family seemed to divine
my friendly intent. Suddenly ceasing their
cries and threats, they perched quietly within reach of my hand, and watched me in my
work of manumission. This, owing to the
fluttering terror of the prisoners, was an
affair of some delicacy ; but erelong I was
rewarded by seeing one of them fly away to
a neighboring tree, while the cripple, making

a parachute of his wings, came lightly to the
ground, and hopped off as well as he could
with one leg, obsequiously waited on by his
elders. A week later I had the satisfaction
of meeting him in the pine-walk, in good
spirits, and already so far recovered as to
be able to balance himself with the lame
foot. I have no doubt that in his old age
he accounted for his lameness by some hand-
some story of a wound received at the famous Battle of the Pines, when our tribe,
overcome by numbers, was driven from its
ancient camping-ground. Of late years the
jays have visited us only at intervals ; and
in winter their bright plumage, set off by
the snow, and their cheerful cry, are especially welcome. They would have furnished
Æsop with a fable, for the feathered crest in
which they seem to take so much satisfaction is often their fatal snare. Country boys
make a hole with their finger in the snow-
crust just large enough to admit the jay's
head, and, hollowing it out somewhat beneath, bait it with a few kernels of corn.
The crest slips easily into the trap, but re-

fuses to be pulled out again, and he who
came to feast remains a prey.

Twice have the crow-blackbirds attempted
a settlement in my pines, and twice have the
robins, who claim a right of pre-emption, so
successfully played the part of border-ruf-
fians as to drive them away, — to my great
regret, for they are the best substitute we
have for rooks. At Shady Hill (now, alas!
empty of its so long-loved household) they
build by hundreds, and nothing can be more
cheery than their creaking clatter (like a
convention of old-fashioned tavern-signs) as
they gather at evening to debate in mass
meeting their windy politics, or to gossip
at their tent-doors over the events of the
day. Their port is grave, and their stalk
across the turf as martial as that of a second-
rate ghost in Hamlet. They never meddled
with my corn, so far as I could discover.

For a few years I had crows, but their
nests are an irresistible bait for boys, and
their settlement was broken up. They grew
so wonted as to throw off a great part of
their shyness, and to tolerate my near ap-

proach. One very hot day I stood for some
time within twenty feet of a mother and
three children, who sat on an elm bough
over my head, gasping in the sultry air, and
holding their wings half-spread for coolness.
All birds during the pairing season become
more or less sentimental, and murmur soft
nothings in a tone very unlike the grinding-
organ repetition and loudness of their habitual song. The crow is very comical as a
lover, and to hear him trying to soften his
croak to the proper Saint Preux standard,
has something the effect of a Mississippi
boatman quoting Tennyson. Yet there are
few things to my ear more melodious than
his caw of a clear winter morning as it drops
to you filtered through five hundred fathoms
of crisp blue air. The hostility of all smaller
birds makes the moral character of the crow,
for all his deaconlike demeanor and garb,
somewhat questionable. He could never
sally forth without insult. The golden robins, especially, would chase him as far as I
could follow with my eye, making him duck
clumsily to avoid their importunate bills. I

do not believe, however, that he robbed any nests hereabouts, for the refuse of the gas-works, which, in our free-and-easy community, is allowed to poison the river, supplied him with dead alewives in abundance. I used to watch him making his periodical visits to the salt-marshes and coming back with a fish in his beak to his young savages, who, no doubt, like it in that condition which makes it savory to the Kanakas and other corvine races of men.

Orioles are in great plenty with me. I have seen seven males flashing about the garden at once. A merry crew of them swing their hammocks from the pendulous boughs. During one of these latter years, when the canker-worms stripped our elms as bare as winter, these birds went to the trouble of rebuilding their unroofed nests, and chose for the purpose trees which are safe from those swarming vandals, such as the ash and the button-wood. One year a pair (disturbed, I suppose, elsewhere) built a second nest in an elm, within a few yards of the house. My friend, Edward E. Hale,

told me once that the oriole rejected from
his web all strands of brilliant color, and I
thought it a striking example of that instinct of concealment noticeable in many
birds, though it should seem in this instance
that the nest was amply protected by its
position from all marauders but owls and
squirrels. Last year, however, I had the
fullest proof that Mr. Hale was mistaken.
A pair of orioles built on the lowest trailer
of a weeping elm, which hung within ten
feet of our drawing-room window, and so
low that I could reach it from the ground.
The nest was wholly woven and felted with
ravellings of woollen carpet in which scarlet
predominated. Would the same thing have
happened in the woods ? Or did the nearness of a human dwelling perhaps give the
birds a greater feeling of security ? They
are very bold, by the way, in quest of cord-
age, and I have often watched them strip-
ping the fibrous bark from a honeysuckle
growing over the very door. But, indeed,
all my birds look upon me as if I were a
mere tenant at will, and they were land-

lords. With shame I confess it, I have been
bullied even by a humming-bird. This
spring, as I was cleansing a pear-tree of its
lichens, one of these little zigzagging blurs
came purring toward me, couching his long
bill like a lance, his throat sparkling with
angry fire, to warn me off from a Missouri-
currant whose honey he was sipping. And
many a time he has driven me out of a
flower-bed. This summer, by the way, a
pair of these winged emeralds fastened their
mossy acorn-cup upon a bough of the same
elm which the orioles had enlivened the
year before. We watched all their proceed-
ings from the window through .an opera-
glass, and saw their two nestlings grow from
black needles with a tuft of down at the
lower end, till they whirled away on their
first short experimental flights. They became strong of wing in a surprisingly short
time, and I never saw them or the male bird
after, though the female was regular as usual
in her visits to our petunias and verbenas.
I do not think it ground enough for a gen-
eralization, but in the many times when I

watched the old birds feeding their young,
the mother always alighted, while the father
as uniformly remained upon the wing.

The bobolinks are generally chance visitors, tinkling through the garden in blos-
soming-time, but this year, owing to the
long rains early in the season, their favorite
meadows were flooded, and they were driven
to the upland. So I had a pair of them
domiciled in my grass-field. The male used
to perch in an apple-tree, then in full bloom,
and, while I stood perfectly still close by,
he would circle away, quivering round the
entire field of five acres, with no break in
his song, and settle down again among the
blossoms, to be hurried away almost imme-
diately by a new rapture of music. He had the
volubility of an Italian charlatan at a fair,
and, like him, appeared to be proclaiming the
merits of some quack remedy. *Opodeldoc-
opodeldoc - try -Doctor -Lincoln's -opodeldoc !* he
seemed to repeat over and over again, with
a rapidity that would have distanced the
deftest-tongued Figaro that ever rattled. I
remember Count Gurowski saying once,

with that easy superiority of knowledge
about this country which is the monopoly
of foreigners, that we had no singing-birds!
Well, well, Mr. Hepworth Dixon has found
the typical America in Oneida and Salt
Lake City. Of course, an intelligent European is the best judge of these matters.
The truth is there are more singing-birds
in Europe because there are fewer forests.
These songsters love the neighborhood of
man because hawks and owls are rarer,
while their own food is more abundant.
Most people seem to think, the more trees,
the more birds. Even Châteaubriand, who
first tried the primitive-forest-cure, and
whose description of the wilderness in its
imaginative effects is unmatched, fancies the
"people of the air singing their hymns to
him." So far as my own observation goes,
the farther one penetrates the sombre soli-
tudes of the woods, the more seldom does
he hear the voice of any singing-bird. In
spite of Châteaubriand's minuteness of de-
tail, in spite of that marvellous reverberation of the decrepit tree falling of its own

weight, which he was the first to notice, I cannot help doubting whether he made his way very deep into the wilderness. At any rate, in a letter to Fontanes, written in 1804, he speaks of *mes chevaux paissant à quelque distance*. To be sure Châteaubriand was apt to mount the high horse, and this may have been but an afterthought of the *grand seigneur*, but certainly one would not make much headway on horseback toward the druid fastnesses of the primeval pine.

The bobolinks build in considerable numbers in a meadow within a quarter of a mile of us. A houseless lane passes through the midst of their camp, and in clear westerly weather, at the right season, one may hear a score of them singing at once. When they are breeding, if I chance to pass, one of the male birds always accompanies me like a constable, flitting from post to post of the rail-fence, with a short note of reproof continually repeated, till I am fairly out of the neighborhood. Then he will swing away into the air and run down the wind, gurgling music without stint over the unheeding tussocks of meadow-grass and dark clumps of bulrushes that mark his domain.

We have no bird whose song will match the nightingale's in compass, none whose note is so rich as that of the European blackbird; but for mere rapture I have never heard the bobolink's rival. But his opera-season is a short one. The ground and tree sparrows are our most constant performers. It is now late in August, and one of the latter sings every day and all day long in the garden. Till within a fortnight, a pair of indigo-birds would keep up their lively *duo* for an hour together. While I write, I hear an oriole gay as in June, and the plaintive *may-be* of the goldfinch tells me he is stealing my lettuce-seeds. I know not what the experience of others may have been, but the only bird I have ever heard sing in the night has been the chip-bird. I should say he sang about as often during the darkness as cocks crow. One can hardly help fancying that he sings in his dreams.

> "Father of light, what sunnie seed,
>   What glance of day hast thou confined

Into this bird ?   To all the breed
This busie ray thou hast assigned ;
Their magnetism works all night,
And dreams of Paradise and light."

On second thought, I remember to have
heard the cuckoo strike the hours nearly all
night with the regularity of a Swiss clock.

The dead limbs of our elms, which I spare
to that end, bring us the flicker every summer, and almost daily I hear his wild scream
and laugh close at hand, himself invisible.
He is a shy bird, but a few days ago I had
the satisfaction of studying him through the
blinds as he sat on a tree within a few feet
of me.   Seen so near and at rest, he makes
good his claim to the title of pigeon-wood-
pecker.   Lumberers have a notion that he
is harmful to timber, digging little holes
through the bark to encourage the settlement of insects.   The regular rings of such
perforations which one may see in almost
any apple-orchard seem to give some probability to this theory.   Almost every season
a solitary quail visits us, and, unseen among
the currant-bushes, calls *Bob White, Bob*

White, as if he were playing at hide-and-seek with that imaginary being. A rarer visitant is the turtle-dove, whose pleasant coo (something like the muffled crow of a cock from a coop covered with snow) I have sometimes heard, and whom I once had the good luck to see close by me in the mulberry-tree. The wild-pigeon, once numerous, I have not seen for many years.* Of savage birds, a hen-hawk now and then quarters himself upon us for a few days, sitting sluggish in a tree after a surfeit of poultry. One of them once offered me a near shot from my study-window one drizzly day for several hours. But it was Sunday, and I gave him the benefit of its gracious truce of God.

Certain birds have disappeared from our neighborhood within my memory. I remember when the whippoorwill could be heard in Sweet Auburn. The night-hawk, once common, is now rare. The brown thrush has moved farther up country. For

---

* They made their appearance again this summer (1870).

years I have not seen or heard any of the
larger owls, whose hooting was one of my
boyish terrors.   The cliff-swallow, strange
emigrant, that eastward takes his way, has
come and gone again in my time.   The
bank-swallows, wellnigh innumerable during
my boyhood, no longer frequent the crumbly
cliff of the gravel-pit by the river.   The
barn-swallows, which once swarmed in our
barn, flashing through the dusty sun-streaks
of the mow, have been gone these many
years.   My father would lead me out to see
them gather on the roof, and take counsel
before their yearly migration, as Mr. White
used to see them at Selborne.   *Eheu, fugaces!*
Thank fortune, the swift still glues his nest,
and rolls his distant thunders night and day
in the wide-throated chimneys, still sprinkles
the evening air with his merry twittering.
The populous heronry in Fresh Pond meadows has been wellnigh broken up, but still
a pair or two ·haunt the old home, as the
gypsies of Ellangowan their ruined huts,
and every evening fly over us riverwards,
clearing their throats with a hoarse hawk

as they go, and, in cloudy weather, scarce higher than the tops of the chimneys. Sometimes I have known one to alight in one of our trees, though for what purpose I never could divine. Kingfishers have sometimes puzzled me in the same way, perched at high noon in a pine, springing their watchman's rattle when they flitted away from my curiosity, and seeming to shove their topheavy heads along as a man does a wheelbarrow.

Some birds have left us, I suppose, because the country is growing less wild. I once found a summer duck's nest within quarter of a mile of our house, but such a *trouvaille* would be impossible now as Kidd's treasure. And yet the mere taming of the neighborhood does not quite satisfy me as an explanation. Twenty years ago, on my way to bathe in the river, I saw every day a brace of woodcock, on the miry edge of a spring within a few rods of a house, and constantly visited by thirsty cows. There was no growth of any kind to conceal them, and yet these ordinarily shy birds were almost as indiffer-

ent to my passing as common poultry would
have been. Since bird-nesting has become
scientific, and dignified itself as oölogy, that,
no doubt, is partly to blame for some of our
losses. But some old friends are constant.
Wilson's thrush comes every year to remind
me of that most poetic of ornithologists. He
flits before me through the pine-walk like
the very genius of solitude. A pair of pewees have built immemorially on a jutting
brick in the arched entrance to the ice-house.
Always on the same brick, and never more
than a single pair, though two broods of five
each are raised there every summer. How
do they settle their claim to the homestead ?
By what right of primogeniture ? Once the
children of a man employed about the place
oölogized the nest, and the pewees left us for
a year or two. I felt towards those boys as
the messmates of the Ancient Mariner did
towards him after he had shot the albatross.
But the pewees came back at last, and one
of them is now on his wonted perch, so near
my window that I can hear the click of his
bill as he snaps a fly on the wing with

the unerring precision a stately Trasteverina shows in the capture of her smaller deer. The pewee is the first bird to pipe up in the morning ; and during the early summer he preludes his matutinal ejaculation of *pewee* with a slender whistle, unheard at any other time. He saddens with the season, and, as summer declines, he changes his note to *eheu, pewee !* as if in lamentation. Had he been an Italian bird, Ovid would have had a plaintive tale to tell about him. He is so familiar as often to pursue a fly through the open window into my library.

There is something inexpressibly dear to me in these old friendships of a lifetime. There is scarce a tree of mine but has had, at some time or other, a happy homestead among its boughs, to which I cannot say,

> " Many light hearts and wings,
> Which now be dead, lodged in thy living bowers."

My walk under the pines would lose half its summer charm were I to miss that shy anchorite, the Wilson's thrush, nor hear in haying-time the metallic ring of his song,

that justifies his rustic name of *scythe-whet*.
I protect my game as jealously as an English
squire. If anybody had oölogized a certain
cuckoo's nest I know of (I have a pair in
my garden every year), it would have left
me a sore place in my mind for weeks.   I
love to bring these aborigines back to the
mansuetude they showed to the early voy-
agers, and before (forgive the involuntary
pun) they had grown accustomed to man
and knew his savage ways. And they repay
your kindness with a sweet familiarity too
delicate ever to breed contempt. I have
made a Penn-treaty with them, preferring
that to the Puritan way with the natives,
which converted them to a little Hebraism
and a great deal of Medford rum. If they
will not come near enough to me (as most
of them will), I bring them close with an
opera-glass, — a much better weapon than a
gun. I would not, if I could, convert them
from their pretty pagan ways. The only one
I sometimes have savage doubts about is the
red squirrel. I *think* he oölogizes. I *know*
he eats cherries (we counted five of them at

one time in a single tree, the stones pattering down like the sparse hail that preludes a storm), and that he gnaws off the small end of pears to get at the seeds. He steals the corn from under the noses of my poultry. But what would you have? He will come down upon the limb of the tree I am lying under till he is within a yard of me. He and his mate will scurry up and down the great black-walnut for my diversion, chattering like monkeys. Can I sign his death-warrant who has tolerated me about his grounds so long? Not I. Let them steal, and welcome. I am sure I should, had I had the same bringing up and the same temptation. As for the birds, I do not believe there is one of them but does more good than harm ; and of how many featherless bipeds can this be said?

A GOOD WORD FOR WINTER.

EN scarcely know how beautiful fire
is," says Shelley ; and I am apt to
think there are a good many other
things concerning which their knowledge
might be largely increased without becom-
ing burdensome. Nor are they altogether
reluctant to be taught, — not so reluctant,
perhaps, as unable, — and education is sure
to find one fulcrum ready to her hand by
which to get a purchase on them. For most
of us, I have noticed, are not without an
amiable willingness to assist at any spectacle
or entertainment (loosely so called) for which
no fee is charged at the door. If special
tickets are sent us, another element of pleasure is added in a sense of privilege and pre-

eminence (pitiably scarce in a democracy) so
deeply rooted in human nature that I have
seen people take a strange satisfaction in
being near of kin to the mute chief personage in a funeral. It gave them a moment's
advantage over the rest of us whose grief
was rated at a lower place in the procession.
But the words "admission free" at the
bottom of a handbill, though holding out no
bait of inequality, have yet a singular charm
for many minds, especially in the country.
There is something touching in the constancy with which men attend free lectures,
and in the honest patience with which they
listen to them. He who pays may yawn or
shift testily in his seat, or even go out with
an awful reverberation of criticism, for he has
bought the right to do any or all of these
and paid for it. But gratuitous hearers are
anæsthetized to suffering by a sense of virtue.
They are performing perhaps the noblest,
as it is one of the most difficult, of human
functions in getting Something (no matter
how small) for Nothing. They are not pes-
tered by the awful duty of securing their

money's worth. They are wasting time, to
do which elegantly and without lassitude is
the highest achievement of civilization. If
they are cheated, it is, at worst, only of a
superfluous hour which was rotting on their
hands. Not only is mere amusement made
more piquant, but instruction more palata-
ble, by this universally relished sauce of
gratuity. And if the philosophic observer
finds an object of agreeable contemplation
in the audience, as they listen to a discourse
on the probability of making missionaries
go down better with the Feejee-Islanders by
balancing the hymn-book in one pocket
with a bottle of Worcestershire in the other,
or to a plea for arming the female gorilla
with the ballot, he also takes a friendly interest in the lecturer, and admires the wise
economy of Nature who thus contrives an
ample field of honest labor for her bores.
Even when the insidious hat is passed round
after one of these eleemosynary feasts, the
relish is but heightened by a conscientious
refusal to disturb the satisfaction's completeness with the rattle of a single contributory

penny. So firmly persuaded am I of this
gratis-instinct in our common humanity,
that I believe I could fill a house by adver-
tising a free lecture on Tupper considered as
a philosophic poet, or on my personal recol-
lections of the late James K. Polk. This
being so, I have sometimes wondered that
the peep-shows which Nature provides with
such endless variety for her children, and
to which we are admitted on the bare condition of having eyes, should be so generally
neglected. To be sure, eyes are not so common as people think, or poets would be
plentier, and perhaps also these exhibitions
of hers are cheapened in estimation by the
fact that in enjoying them we are not getting the better of anybody else. Your true
lovers of nature, however, contrive to get even
this solace ; and Wordsworth looking upon
mountains as his own peculiar sweethearts,
was jealous of anybody else who ventured
upon even the most innocent flirtation with
them. As if *such* fellows, indeed, could pre-
tend to that nicer sense of what-d'ye-call-it
which was so remarkable in him ! Marry

come up ! Mountains, no doubt, may inspire a profounder and more exclusive passion,
but on the whole I am not sorry to have
been born and bred among more domestic
scenes, where I can be hospitable without a
pang. I am going to ask you presently to
take potluck with me at a board where Winter shall supply whatever there is of cheer.

I think the old fellow has hitherto had
scant justice done him in the main. We
make him the symbol of old age or death,
and think we have settled the matter. As if
old age were never kindly as well as frosty ;
as if it had no reverend graces of its own as
good in their way as the noisy impertinence of
childhood, the elbowing self-conceit of youth,
or the pompous mediocrity of middle life !
As if there were anything discreditable in
death, or nobody had ever longed for it! Suppose we grant that Winter is the sleep of the
year, what then ? I take it upon me to say
that his dreams are finer than the best reality
of his waking rivals.

"Sleep, Silence' child, the father of soft Rest,"

is a very agreeable acquaintance, and most
of us are better employed in his company
than anywhere else. For my own part, I
think Winter a pretty wide-awake old boy,
and his bluff sincerity and hearty ways are
more congenial to my mood, and more wholesome for me, than any charms of which his
rivals are capable. Spring is a fickle mistress, who either does not know her own
mind, or is so long in making it up, whether
you shall have her or not have her, that
one gets tired at last of her pretty miffs and
reconciliations. You go to her to be cheered
up a bit, and ten to one catch her in the
sulks, expecting you to find enough good-
humor for both. After she has become
Mrs. Summer she grows a little more staid
in her demeanor ; and her abundant table,
where you are sure to get the earliest fruits
and vegetables of the season, is a good foun-
dation for steady friendship ; but she has
lost that delicious aroma of maidenhood, and
what was delicately rounded grace in the
girl gives more than hints of something like
redundance in the matron. Autumn is the

poet of the family. He gets you up a splendor that you would say was made out of real sunset; but it is nothing more than a few hectic leaves, when all is done. He is but a sentimentalist, after all; a kind of Lamartine whining along the ancestral avenues he has made bare timber of, and begging a contribution of good-spirits from your own savings to keep him in countenance. But Winter has his delicate sensibilities too, only he does not make them as good as indelicate by thrusting them forever in your face. He is a better poet than Autumn, when he has a mind, but, like a truly great one as he is, he brings you down to your bare manhood, and bids you understand him out of that, with no adventitious helps of association, or he will none of you. He does not touch those melancholy chords on which Autumn is as great a master as Heine. Well, is there no such thing as thrumming on them and maundering over them till they get out of tune, and you wish some manly hand would crash through them and leave them dangling brokenly forever? Take Winter as you find

him, and he turns out to be a thoroughly
honest fellow, with no nonsense in him, and
tolerating none in you, which is a great comfort in the long run. He is not what they
call a genial critic ; but bring a real man
along with you, and you will find there is a
crabbed generosity about the old cynic that
you would not exchange for all the creamy
concessions of Autumn. " Season of mists
and mellow fruitfulness," quotha ? That 's
just it ; Winter soon blows your head clear
of fog and makes you see things as they are ;
I thank him for it ! The truth is, between
ourselves, I have a very good opinion of the
whole family, who always welcome me without making me feel as if I were too much of
a poor relation. There ought to be some
kind of distance, never so little, you know,
to give the true relish. They are as good
company, the worst of them, as any I know,
and I am not a little flattered by a condescension from any one of them ; but I happen to hold Winter's retainer, this time, and,
like an honest advocate, am bound to make
as good a showing as I can for him, even if

it cost a few slurs upon the rest of the household. Moreover, Winter is coming, and one would like to get on the blind side of him.

The love of Nature in and for herself, or as a mirror for the moods of the mind, is a modern thing. The fleeing to her as an escape from man was brought into fashion by Rousseau ; for his prototype Petrarch, though he had a taste for pretty scenery, had a true antique horror for the grander aspects of nature. He got once to the top of Mont Ventoux, but it is very plain that he did not enjoy it. Indeed, it is only within a century or so that the search after the picturesque has been a safe employment. It is not so even now in Greece or Southern Italy. Where the Anglo-Saxon carves his cold fowl, and leaves the relics of his picnic, the ancient or mediæval man might be pretty confident that some ruffian would try the edge of his knife on a chicken of the Platonic sort, and leave more precious bones as an offering to the genius of the place. The ancients were certainly more social than we, though that, perhaps, was natural enough, when a good part of the world was still covered with forest. They huddled together in cities as well for safety as to keep their minds warm. The Romans had a fondness for country life, but they had fine roads, and Rome was always within easy reach. The author of the Book of Job is the earliest I know of who showed any profound sense of the moral meaning of the outward world ; and I think none has approached him since, though Wordsworth comes nearest with the first two books of the "Prelude." But their feeling is not precisely of the kind I speak of as modern, and which gave rise to what is called descriptive poetry. Chaucer opens his Clerk's Tale with a bit of landscape admirable for its large style, and as well composed as any Claude.

> " There is right at the west end of Itaille,
>   Down at the root of Vesulus the cold,
>   A lusty plain abundant of vitaille,
>   Where many a tower and town thou mayst be-
>   hold,
>   That founded were in time of fathers old,
>   And many an other délectable sight ;
>   And Salucës this noble country hight."

What an airy precision of touch there is
here, and what a sure eye for the points of
character in landscape ! But the picture is
altogether subsidiary. No doubt the works of
Salvator Rosa and Gaspar Poussin show that
there must have been some amateur taste for
the grand and terrible in scenery ; but the
British poet Thomson ("sweet-souled" is
Wordsworth's apt word) was the first to do
with words what they had done partially
with colors. He was turgid, no good me-
trist, and his English is like a translation
from one of those poets who wrote in Latin
after it was dead ; but he was a man of sincere genius, and not only English, but European literature is largely in his debt. He
was the inventor of cheap amusement for the
million, to be had of All-out-doors for the
asking. It was his impulse which unconsciously gave direction to Rousseau, and it is
to the school of Jean Jacques that we owe
St. Pierre, Cowper, Châteaubriand, Wordsworth, Byron, Lamartine, George Sand, Rus-
kin, — the great painters of ideal landscape.

So long as men had slender means, wheth-

er of keeping out cold or checkmating it
with artificial heat, Winter was an unwelcome guest, especially in the country. There
he was the bearer of a *lettre de cachet*, which
shut its victims in solitary confinement with
few resources but to boose round the fire and
repeat ghost-stories, which had lost all their
freshness and none of their terror.   To go to
bed was to lie awake of cold, with an added
shudder of fright whenever a loose casement
or a waving curtain chose to give you the
goose-flesh. Bussy Rabutin, in one of his
letters, gives us a notion how uncomfort-
able it was in the country, with green wood,
smoky chimneys, and doors and windows that
thought it was their duty to make the wind
whistle, not to keep it out. With fuel so
dear, it could not have been much better
in the city, to judge by Ménage's warning
against the danger of our dressing-gowns taking fire, while we cuddle too closely over the
sparing blaze. The poet of Winter himself
is said to have written in bed, with his hand
through a hole in the blanket ; and we may
suspect that it was the warmth quite as

much as the company that first drew men
together at the coffee-house. Coleridge, in
January, 1800, writes to Wedgewood : " I
am sitting by a fire in a rug great-coat. . . . .
It is most barbarously cold, and you, I fear,
can shield yourself from it only by perpetual
imprisonment." This thermometrical view
of winter is, I grant, a depressing one ; for
I think there is nothing so demoralizing as
cold. I know of a boy who, when his father,
a bitter economist, was brought home dead,
said only, " Now we can burn as much wood
as we like." I would not off-hand prophesy
the gallows for that boy. I remember with
a shudder a pinch I got from the cold once
in a railroad-car. A born fanatic of fresh
air, I found myself glad to see the windows
hermetically sealed by the freezing vapor
of our breath, and plotted the assassination
of the conductor every time he opened the
door. I felt myself sensibly barbarizing,
and would have shared Colonel Jack's bed
in the ash-hole of the glass-furnace with a
grateful heart. Since then I have had more
charity for the prevailing ill-opinion of win-

ter. It was natural enough that Ovid should measure the years of his exile in Pontus by the number of winters.

> Ut sumus in Ponto, ter frigore constitit Ister,
> Facta est Euxini dura ter unda maris :

> Thrice hath the cold bound Ister fast, since I
> In Pontus was, thrice Euxine's wave made hard.

Jubinal has printed an Anglo-Norman piece of doggerel in which Winter and Summer dispute which is the better man. It is not without a kind of rough and inchoate humor, and I like it because old Whitebeard gets tolerably fair play. The jolly old fellow boasts of his rate of living, with that contempt of poverty which is the weak spot in the burly English nature.

> Jà Dieu ne place que me avyenge
> Que ne face plus honour
> Et plus despenz en un soul jour
> Que vus en tote vostre vie :

> Now God forbid it hap to me
> That I make not more great display,
> And spend more in a single day
> Than you can do in all your life.

The best touch, perhaps, is Winter's claim
for credit as a mender of the highways,
which was not without point when every
road in Europe was a quagmire during a
good part of the year unless it was bottomed
on some remains of Roman engineering.

> Je su, fet-il, seignur et mestre
> Et à bon droit le dey estre,
> Quant de la bowe face caucé
> Par un petit de geelé :
>
> Master and lord I am, says he,
> And of good right so ought to be,
> Since I make causeys, safely crost,
> Of mud, with just a pinch of frost. ·

But there is no recognition of Winter as the
best of outdoor company.

Even Emerson, an open-air man, and a
bringer of it, if ever any, confesses,

> " The frost-king ties my fumbling feet,
> Sings in my ear, my hands are stones,
> Curdles the blood to the marble bones,
> Tugs at the heartstrings, numbs the sense,
> And hems in life with narrowing fence."

Winter was literally "the inverted year," as Thomson called him ; for such entertainments as could be had must be got within doors. What cheerfulness there was in brumal verse was that of Horace's *dissolve frigus ligna super foco large reponens*, so pleasantly associated with the cleverest scene in Roderick Random. This is the tone of that poem of Walton's friend Cotton, which won the praise of Wordsworth : —

> "Let us home,
> Our mortal enemy is come ;
> Winter and all his blustering train
> Have made a voyage o'er the main.
>
> . . . . .
>
> "Fly, fly, the foe advances fast ;
> Into our fortress let us haste,
> Where all the roarers of the north
> Can neither storm nor starve us forth.
>
> "There underground a magazine
> Of sovereign juice is cellared in,
> Liquor that will the siege maintain
> Should Phœbus ne'er return again.
>
> . . . . .
>
> "Whilst we together jovial sit
> Careless, and crowned with mirth and wit,

Where, though bleak winds confine us home,
Our fancies round the world shall roam."

Thomson's view of Winter is also, on the
whole, a hostile one, though he does justice
to his grandeur.

"Thus Winter falls,
A heavy gloom oppressive o'er the world,
Through Nature shedding influence malign."

He finds his consolations, like Cotton, in the
house, though more refined : —

" While without
The ceaseless winds blow ice, be my retreat
Between the groaning forest and the shore
Beat by the boundless multitude of waves,
A rural, sheltered, solitary scene,
Where ruddy fire and beaming tapers join
To cheer the gloom.   There studious let me sit
And hold high converse with the mighty dead."

Doctor Akenside, a man to be spoken of with
respect, follows Thomson.   With him, too,
"Winter desolates the year," and

" How pleasing wears the wintry night
Spent with the old illustrious dead !
While by the taper's trembling light

I seem those awful scenes to tread
Where chiefs or legislators lie," &c.

Akenside had evidently been reading
Thomson.   He had the conceptions of a
great poet with less faculty than many a
little one, and is one of those versifiers of
whom it is enough to say that we are always
willing to break him off in the middle with
an &c., well knowing that what follows is
but the coming-round again of what went
before, marching in a circle with the cheap
numerosity of a stage-army.   In truth, it
is no wonder that the short days of that
cloudy northern climate should have added
to winter a gloom borrowed of the mind.
We hardly know, till we have experienced
the contrast, how sensibly our winter is alle-
viated by the longer daylight and the pel-
lucid atmosphere.   I once spent a winter in
Dresden, a southern climate compared with
England, and really almost lost my respect
for the sun when I saw him groping among
the chimney-pots opposite my windows as
he described his impoverished arc in the
sky.   The enforced seclusion of the season

makes it the time for serious study and oc-
cupations that demand fixed incomes of unbroken time. This is why Milton said "that
his vein never happily flowed but from the
autumnal equinox to the vernal," though in
his twentieth year he had written, on the return of spring, —

Fallor ? an et nobis redeunt in carmina vires
Ingeniumque mihi munere veris adest ?

Err I ? or do the powers of song return
To me, and genius too, the gifts of Spring ?

Goethe, so far as I remember, was the first
to notice the cheerfulness of snow in sunshine. His *Harz-reise im Winter* gives no
hint of it, for that is a diluted reminiscence
of Greek tragic choruses and the Book of
Job in nearly equal parts. In one of the
singularly interesting and characteristic letters to Frau von Stein, however, written
during the journey, he says : "It is beautiful indeed ; the mist heaps itself together in
light snow-clouds, the sun looks through,
and the snow over everything gives back a

feeling of gayety." But I find in Cowper
the first recognition of a general amiability
in Winter. The gentleness of his temper,
and the wide charity of his sympathies, made
it natural for him to find good in everything
except the human heart. A dreadful creed
distilled from the darkest moments of dyspeptic solitaries compelled him against his
will to see in *that* the one evil thing made
by a God whose goodness is over all his
works. Cowper's two walks in the morning and noon of a winter's day are delightful, so long as he contrives to let himself be
happy in the graciousness of the landscape.
Your muscles grow springy, and your lungs
dilate with the crisp air as you walk along
with him. You laugh with him at the gro-
tesque shadow of your legs lengthened across
the snow by the just-risen sun. I know
nothing that gives a purer feeling of outdoor exhilaration than the easy verses of this
escaped hypochondriac. But Cowper also
preferred his sheltered garden-walk to those
robuster joys, and bitterly acknowledged the
depressing influence of the darkened year.

In December, 1780, he writes : " At this
season of the year, and in this gloomy un-
comfortable climate, it is no easy matter for
the owner of a mind like mine to divert it
from sad subjects, and to fix it upon such
as may administer to its amusement." Or
was it because he was writing to the dreadful Newton ? Perhaps his poetry bears truer
witness to his habitual feeling, for it is only
there that poets disenthral themselves of their
reserve and become fully possessed of their
greatest charm, — the power of being franker
than other men. In the Third Book of the
Task he boldly affirms his preference of the
country to the city even in winter : —

"But are not wholesome airs, though unperfumed
 By roses, and clear suns, though scarcely felt,
 And groves, if inharmonious, yet secure
 From clamor, and whose very silence charms,
 To be preferred to smoke ? . . . .
 They would be, were not madness in the head
 And folly in the heart ; were England now
 What England was, plain, hospitable kind,
 And undebauched."

The conclusion shows, however, that he
was thinking mainly of fireside delights, not

of the blusterous companionship of nature. This appears even more clearly in the Fourth Book : —

"O Winter, ruler of the inverted year";

but I cannot help interrupting him to say how pleasant it always is to track poets through the gardens of their predecessors and find out their likings by a flower snapped off here and there to garnish their own nosegays. Cowper had been reading Thomson, and "the inverted year" pleased his fancy with its suggestion of that starry wheel of the zodiac moving round through its spaces infinite. He could not help loving a handy Latinism (especially with elision beauty added), any more than Gray, any more than Wordsworth, — on the sly. But the member for Olney has the floor : —

"O Winter, ruler of the inverted year,
   Thy scattered hair with sleet like ashes filled,
   Thy breath congealed upon thy lips, thy cheeks
   Fringed with a beard made white with other snows
   Than those of age, thy forehead wrapt in clouds,
   A leafless branch thy sceptre, and thy throne
   A sliding car, indebted to no wheels,

But urged by storms along its slippery way,
I love thee all unlovely as thou seem'st,
And dreaded as thou art ! Thou hold'st the sun
A prisoner in the yet undawning east,
Shortening his journey between morn and noon,
And hurrying him, impatient of his stay,
Down to the rosy west, but kindly still
Compensating his loss with added hours
Of social converse and instructive ease,
And gathering at short notice, in one group,
The family dispersed, and fixing thought,
Not less dispersed by daylight and its cares.
I crown thee king of intimate delights,
Fireside enjoyments, homeborn happiness,
And all the comforts that the lowly roof
Of undisturbed Retirement, and the hours
Of long uninterrupted evening know."

I call this a good *human* bit of writing,
imaginative, too, — not so flushed, not so
. . . . highfaluting (let me dare the odious
word !) as the modern style since poets have
got hold of a theory that imagination is
common-sense turned inside out, and not
common-sense sublimed, — but wholesome,
masculine, and strong in the simplicity of a
mind wholly occupied with its theme. To

me Cowper is still the best of our descriptive poets for every-day wear. And what unobtrusive skill he has! How he heightens, for example, your sense of winter-evening seclusion, by the twanging horn of the postman on the bridge! That horn has rung in my ears ever since I first heard it, during the consulate of the second Adams. Wordsworth strikes a deeper note; but does it not sometimes come over one (just the least in the world) that one would give anything for a bit of nature pure and simple, without quite so strong a flavor of W. W.? W. W. is, of course, sublime and all that — but! For my part, I will make a clean breast of it, and confess that I can't look at a mountain without fancying the late laureate's gigantic Roman nose thrust between me and it, and thinking of Dean Swift's profane version of *Romanos rerum dominos* into *Roman nose! a rare un! dom your nose!* But do I judge verses, then, by the impression made on me by the man who wrote them? Not so fast, my good friend, but, for good or evil, the character and its intellectual product are inextricably interfused.

If I remember aright, Wordsworth himself (except in his magnificent skating-scene
in the "Prelude") has not much to say for
winter out of doors. I cannot recall any
picture by him of a snow-storm. The
reason may possibly be that in the Lake
Country even the winter storms bring rain
rather than snow. He was thankful for the
Christmas visits of Crabb Robinson, because
they "helped him through the winter."
His only hearty praise of winter is when, as
Général Février, he defeats the French : —

"Humanity, delighting to behold
A fond reflection of her own decay,
Hath painted Winter like a traveller old,
Propped on a staff, and, through the sullen day,
In hooded mantle, limping o'er the plain
As though his weakness were disturbed by pain :
Or, if a juster fancy should allow
An undisputed symbol of command,
The chosen sceptre is a withered bough
Infirmly grasped within a withered hand.
These emblems suit the helpless and forlorn ;
But mighty Winter the device shall scorn."

The Scottish poet Grahame, in his "Sabbath," says manfully : —

> " Now is the time
> To visit Nature in her grand attire";

and he has one little picture which no other poet has surpassed : —

> " High-ridged the whirlëd drift has almost reached
> The powdered keystone of the churchyard porch :
> Mute hangs the hooded bell; the tombs lie buried."

Even in our own climate, where the sun shows his winter face as long and as brightly as in Central Italy, the seduction of the chimney-corner is apt to predominate in the mind over the severer satisfactions of muffled fields and penitential woods. The very title of Whittier's delightful "Snow-Bound" shows what *he* was thinking of, though he does vapor a little about digging out paths. The verses of Emerson, perfect as a Greek fragment (despite the archaism of a dissyllabic fire), which he has chosen for his epigraph, tell us, too, how the

> " Housemates sit
> Around the radiant fireplace, enclosed
> In a tumultuous privacy of storm."

They are all in a tale. It is always the
tristis Hiems of Virgil. Catch one of them
having a kind word for old Barbe Fleurie,
unless he whines through some cranny, like
a beggar, to heighten their enjoyment while
they toast their slippered toes. I grant
there is a keen relish of contrast about
the bickering flame as it gives an emphasis
beyond Gherardo della Notte to loved faces,
or kindles the gloomy gold of volumes
scarce less friendly, especially when a tempest is blundering round the house. Wordsworth has a fine touch that brings home to
us the comfortable contrast of without and
within, during a storm at night, and the
passage is highly characteristic of a poet
whose inspiration always has an undertone
of *bourgeois:* —

> " How touching, when, at midnight, sweep
> Snow-muffled winds, and all is dark,
> To hear, — and sink again to sleep ! "

J. H., one of those choice poets who will
not tarnish their bright fancies by publica-
tion, always insists on a snow-storm as essen-

tial to the true atmosphere of whist. Mrs.
Battles, in her famous rule for the game, im-
plies winter, and would doubtless have added
tempest, if it could be had for the asking. For
a good solid read also, into the small hours,
there is nothing like that sense of safety
against having your evening laid waste,
which Euroclydon brings, as he bellows
down the chimney, making your fire gasp,
or rustles snow-flakes against the pane with
a sound more soothing than silence. Emerson, as he is apt to do, not only hit the nail
on the head, but drove it home, in that last
phrase of the " tumultuous privacy."

But I would exchange this, and give something to boot, for the privilege of walking
out into the vast blur of a north-northeast
snow-storm, and getting a strong draught on
the furnace within, by drawing the first furrows through its sandy drifts. I love those

> " Noontide twilights which snow makes
> With tempest of the blinding flakes."

If the wind veer too much toward the east,
you get the heavy snow that gives a true

Alpine slope to the boughs of your ever-
greens, and traces a skeleton of your elms in
white ; but you must have plenty of north
in your gale if you want those driving nettles
of frost that sting the cheeks to a crimson
manlier than that of fire.   During the great
storm of two winters ago, the most robustious
periwig-pated fellow of late years, I waded
and floundered a couple of miles through the
whispering night, and brought home that
feeling of expansion we have after being in
good company.   " Great things doeth He
which we cannot comprehend ; for he saith
to the snow, ' Be thou on the earth.' "

There is admirable snow scenery in Judd's
" Margaret," but some one has confiscated
my copy of that admirable book, and, perhaps, Homer's picture of a snow-storm is the
best yet in its large simplicity : —

" And as in winter-time, when Jove his cold sharp
    javelins throws
  Amongst us mortals, and is moved to white the
    earth with snows,
  The winds asleep, he freely pours till highest
    prominents,

Hill-tops, low meadows, and the fields that crown
  with most contents
The toils of men, seaports and shores, are hid,
  and every place,
But floods, that fair snow's tender flakes, as their
  own brood, embrace."

Chapman, after all, though he makes very free with him, comes nearer Homer than anybody else. There is nothing in the original of that fair snow's tender flakes, but neither Pope nor Cowper could get out of their heads the Psalmist's tender phrase, " He giveth his snow like wool," for which also Homer affords no hint. Pope talks of " dissolving fleeces," and Cowper of a " fleecy mantle." But David is nobly simple, while Pope is simply nonsensical, and Cowper pretty. If they must have prettiness, Martial would have supplied them with it in his

Densum tacitarum vellus aquarum,

which is too pretty, though I fear it would have pleased Dr. Donne. Eustathius of Thessalonica calls snow ὕδωρ ἐρίωδες, woolly water, which a poor old French poet, Godeau, has amplified into this : —

Lorsque la froidure inhumaine
De leur verd ornement depouille les forêts
Sous une neige épaisse il couvre les guérets,
Et la neige a pour eux la chaleur de la laine.

In this, as in Pope's version of the passage in
Homer, there is, at least, a sort of suggestion
of snow-storm in the blinding drift of words.
But, on the whole, if one would know what
snow is, I should advise him not to hunt up
what the poets have said about it, but to look
at the sweet miracle itself.

The preludings of Winter are as beautiful
as those of Spring. In a gray December
day, when, as the farmers say, it is too cold
to snow, his numbed fingers will let fall
doubtfully a few star-shaped flakes, the snow-
drops and anemones that harbinger his more
assured reign. Now, and now only, may be
seen, heaped on the horizon's eastern edge,
those "blue clouds" from forth which
Shakespeare says that Mars "doth pluck the
masoned turrets." Sometimes also, when
the sun is low, you will see a single cloud
trailing a flurry of snow along the southern hills in a wavering fringe of purple.

And when at last the real snow-storm comes,
it leaves the earth with a virginal look on
it that no other of the seasons can rival, —
compared with which, indeed, they seem
soiled and vulgar.

And what is there in nature so beautiful
as the next morning after such confusion of
the elements ? Night has no silence like
this of busy day. All the batteries of noise
are spiked. We see the movement of life as
a deaf man sees it, a mere wraith of the
clamorous existence that inflicts itself on our
ears when the ground is bare. The earth is
clothed in innocence as a garment. Every
wound of the landscape is healed ; whatever
was stiff has been sweetly rounded as the
breasts of Aphrodite ; what was unsightly
has been covered gently with a soft splendor,
as if, Cowley would have said, Nature had
cleverly let fall her handkerchief to hide it.
If the Virgin (*Nôtre Dame de la neige*) were
to come back, here is an earth that would
not bruise her foot nor stain it.   It is

> " The fanned snow
> That 's bolted by the northern blasts twice o'er,"—

Soffiata e stretta dai venti Schiavi,
Winnowed and packed by the Sclavonian winds, —

packed so hard sometimes on hill-slopes that
it will bear your weight. What grace is in
all the curves, as if every one of them had
been swept by that inspired thumb of Phid-
ias's journeyman !

Poets have fancied the footprints of the
wind in those light ripples that sometimes
scurry across smooth water with a sudden
blur. But on this gleaming hush the aerial
deluge has left plain marks of its course ;
and in gullies through which it rushed tor-
rent-like, the eye finds its bed irregularly
scooped like that of a brook in hard beach-
sand, or, in more sheltered spots, traced with
outlines like those left by the sliding edges
of the surf upon the shore. The air, after
all, is only an infinitely thinner kind of
water, such as I suppose we shall have to
drink when the state does her whole duty as
a moral reformer. Nor is the wind the only
thing whose trail you will notice on this
sensitive surface. You will find that you

have more neighbors and night visitors than
you dreamed of. Here is the dainty footprint of a cat ; here a dog has looked in on
you like an amateur watchman to see if all is
right, slumping clumsily about in the mealy
treachery. And look ! before you were up
in the morning, though you were a punctual
courtier at the sun's levee, here has been a
squirrel zigzagging to and fro like a hound
gathering the scent, and some tiny bird
searching for unimaginable food, — perhaps
for the tinier creature, whatever it is, that
drew this slender continuous trail like those
made on the wet beach by light borderers of
the sea. The earliest autographs were as
frail as these. Poseidon traced his lines, or
giant birds made their mark, on preadamite
sea-margins ; and the thunder-gust left the
tear-stains of its sudden passion there ; nay,
we have the signatures of delicatest fern-
leaves on the soft ooze of æons that dozed
away their dreamless leisure before conscious-
ness came upon the earth with man. Some
whim of nature locked them fast in stone
for us after-thoughts of creation. Which of

us shall leave a footprint as imperishable as
that of the ornithorhyncus, or much more
so than that of these Bedouins of the snow-
desert ?   Perhaps it was only because the
ripple and the rain-drop and the bird were
not thinking of themselves, that they had
such luck.   The chances of immortality de-
pend very much on that.   How often have
we not seen poor mortals, dupes of a season's
notoriety, carving their names on seeming-
solid rock of merest beach-sand, whose feeble
hold on memory shall be washed away by
the next wave of fickle opinion!   Well, well,
honest Jacques, there are better things to be
found in the snow than sermons.

The snow that falls damp comes commonly
in larger flakes from windless skies, and is
the prettiest of all to watch from under cover.
This is the kind Homer had in mind; and
Dante, who had never read him, compares
the *dilatate falde*, the flaring flakes, of his
fiery rain, to those of snow among the mountains without wind.   This sort of snowfall
has no fight in it, and does not challenge you
to a wrestle like that which drives well from

the northward, with all moisture thoroughly
winnowed out of it by the frosty wind.
Burns, who was more out of doors than most
poets, and whose barefoot Muse got the color
in her cheeks by vigorous exercise in all
weathers, was thinking of this drier deluge,
when he speaks of the "whirling drift," and
tells how

> "Chanticleer
> Shook off the powthery snaw."

But the damper and more deliberate falls
have a choice knack at draping the trees;
and about eaves or stone-walls, wherever,
indeed, the evaporation is rapid, and it finds
a chance to cling, it will build itself out in
curves of wonderful beauty. I have seen
one of these dumb waves, thus caught in the
act of breaking, curl four feet beyond the
edge of my roof and hang there for days, as
if Nature were too well pleased with her
work to let it crumble from its exquisite
pause. After such a storm, if you are lucky
enough to have even a sluggish ditch for
a neighbor, be sure to pay it a visit. You
will find its banks corniced with what seems

precipitated light, and the dark current down below gleams as if with an inward lustre. Dull of motion as it is, you never saw water that seemed alive before. It has a brightness, like that of the eyes of some smaller animals, which gives assurance of life, but of a life foreign and unintelligible.

A damp snow-storm often turns to rain, and, in our freakish climate, the wind will whisk sometimes into the northwest so suddenly as to plate all the trees with crystal before it has swept the sky clear of its last cobweb of cloud. Ambrose Philips, in a poetical epistle from Copenhagen to the Earl of Dorset, describes this strange confectionery of Nature, — for such, I am half ashamed to say, it always seems to me, recalling the " glorified sugar-candy " of Lamb's first night at the theatre. It has an artificial air, altogether beneath the grand artist of the atmosphere, and besides does too much mischief to the trees for a philodendrist to take unmixed pleasure in it. Perhaps it deserves a poet like Philips, who really loved Nature and yet liked her to be mighty fine, as Pepys

would say, with a heightening of powder and
rouge : —

" And yet but lately have I seen e'en here
The winter in a lovely dress appear.
Ere yet the clouds let fall the treasured snow,
Or winds begun through hazy skies to blow,
At evening a keen eastern breeze arose,
And the descending rain unsullied froze.
Soon as the silent shades of night withdrew,
The ruddy noon disclosed at once to view
The face of Nature in a rich disguise,
And brightened every object to my eyes ;
For every shrub, and every blade of grass,
And every pointed thorn, seemed wrought in glass ;
In pearls and rubies rich the hawthorns show,
And through the ice the crimson berries glow ;
The thick-sprung reeds, which watery marshes yield,
Seem polished lances in a hostile field ;
The stag in limpid currents with surprise
Sees crystal branches on his forehead rise ;
The spreading oak, the beech, the towering pine,
Glazed over in the freezing ether shine ;
The frighted birds the rattling branches shun,
Which wave and glitter in the distant sun,
When, if a sudden gust of wind arise,
The brittle forest into atoms flies,
The crackling wood beneath the tempest bends
And in a spangled shower the prospect ends."

It is not uninstructive to see how tolerable
Ambrose is, so long as he sticks manfully
to what he really saw.   The moment he
undertakes to improve on Nature he sinks
into the mere court poet, and we surrender
him to the jealousy of Pope without a sigh.
His "rattling branches" and "crackling forest" are good, as truth always is after a fashion ; but what shall we say of that dreadful
stag which, there is little doubt, he valued
above all the rest, because it was purely his
own ?

The damper snow tempts the amateur
architect and sculptor.   His Pentelicus has
been brought to his very door, and if there
are boys to be had (whose company beats all
other recipes for prolonging life) a middle-
aged Master of the Works will knock the
years off his account and make the family
Bible seem a dealer in foolish fables, by a
few hours given heartily to this business.
First comes the Sisyphean toil of rolling the
clammy balls till they refuse to budge farther.   Then, if you would play the statuary,
they are piled one upon the other to the

proper height ; or if your aim be masonry,
whether of house or fort, they must be
squared and beaten solid with the shovel.
The material is capable of very pretty effects,
and your young companions meanwhile are
unconsciously learning lessons in æsthetics.
From the feeling of satisfaction with which
one squats on the damp floor of his extem-
porized dwelling, I have been led to think
that the backwoodsman must get a sweeter
savor of self-reliance from the house his own
hands have built than Bramante or Sanso-
vino could ever give. Perhaps the fort is
the best thing, for it calls out more masculine qualities and adds the cheer of battle
with that dumb artillery which gives pain
enough to test pluck without risk of serious
hurt. Already, as I write, it is twenty-odd
years ago. The balls fly thick and fast.
The uncle defends the waist-high ramparts
against a storm of nephews, his breast plas-
tered with decorations like another Radet-
sky's. How well I recall the indomitable
good-humor under fire of him who fell in
the front at Ball's Bluff, the silent perti-

nacity of the gentle scholar who got his last
hurt at Fair Oaks, the ardor in the charge of
the gallant gentleman who, with the death-
wound in his side, headed his brigade at
Cedar Creek! How it all comes back, and
they never come! I cannot again be the
Vauban of fortresses in the innocent snow,
but I shall never see children moulding their
clumsy giants in it without longing to help.
It was a pretty fancy of the young Vermont
sculptor to make his first essay in this eva-
nescent material. Was it a figure of Youth, I
wonder? Would it not be well if all artists
could begin in stuff as perishable, to melt
away when the sun of prosperity began to
shine, and leave nothing behind but the gain
of practised hands? It is pleasant to fancy
that Shakespeare served his apprenticeship at
this trade, and owed to it that most pathetic
of despairing wishes, —

> "O, that I were a mockery-king of snow,
> Standing before the sun of Bolingbroke,
> To melt myself away in water-drops!"

I have spoken of the exquisite curves of
snow surfaces. Not less rare are the tints of

which they are capable, — the faint blue of
the hollows, for the shadows in snow are
always blue, and the tender rose of higher
points, as you stand with your back to the
setting sun and look upward across the soft
rondure of a hillside. I have seen within a
mile of home effects of color as lovely as
any iridescence of the Silberhorn after sundown. Charles II., who never said a foolish
thing, gave the English climate the highest
praise when he said that it allowed you more
hours out of doors than any other, and I
think our winter may fairly make the same
boast as compared with the rest of the year.
Its still mornings, with the thermometer
near zero, put a premium on walking. There
is more sentiment in turf, perhaps, and it is
more elastic to the foot ; its silence, too, is
wellnigh as congenial with meditation as that
of fallen pine-tassel ; but for exhilaration
there is nothing like a stiff snow-crust that
creaks like a cricket at every step, and com-
municates its own sparkle to the senses.
The air you drink is *frappé*, all its grosser
particles precipitated, and the dregs of your

blood with them. A purer current mounts
to the brain, courses sparkling through it,
and rinses it thoroughly of all dejected stuff.
There is nothing left to breed an exhalation
of ill-humor or despondency. They say that
this rarefied atmosphere has lessened the
capacity of our lungs. Be it so. Quart-pots
are for muddier liquor than nectar. To me,
the city in winter is infinitely dreary, — the
sharp street-corners have such a chill in them,
and the snow so soon loses its maidenhood
to become a mere drab, — "doing shameful
things," as Steele says of politicians, "without being ashamed." I pine for the Quaker
purity of my country landscape. I am
speaking, of course, of those winters that
are not niggardly of snow, as ours too often
are, giving us a gravelly dust instead. Nothing can be unsightlier than those piebald
fields where the coarse brown hide of Earth
shows through the holes of her ragged
ermine. But even when there is abundance
of snow, I find as I grow older that there
are not so many good crusts as there used to
be. When I first observed this, I rashly set

it to the account of that general degeneracy
in nature (keeping pace with the same melancholy phenomenon in man) which forces
itself upon the attention and into the philosophy of middle life. But happening once to
be weighed, it occurred to me that an arch
which would bear fifty pounds could hardly
be blamed for giving way under more than
three times the weight. I have sometimes
thought that if theologians would remember
this in their arguments, and consider that the
man may slump through, with no fault of
his own, where the boy would have skimmed
the surface in safety, it would be better for
all parties. However, when you *do* get a
crust that will bear, and know any brooklet
that runs down a hillside, be sure to go and
take a look at him, especially if your crust is
due, as it commonly is, to a cold snap following eagerly on a thaw. You will never find
him so cheerful. As he shrank away after
the last thaw, he built for himself the most
exquisite caverns of ice to run through, if
not " measureless to man" like those of
Alph, the sacred river, yet perhaps more

pleasing for their narrowness than those for
their grandeur. What a cunning silversmith
is Frost ! The rarest workmanship of Delhi
or Genoa copies him but clumsily, as if the
fingers of all other artists were thumbs.
Fernwork and lacework and filigree in endless variety, and under it all the water tin-
kles like a distant guitar, or drums like a
tambourine, or gurgles like the Tokay of an
anchorite's dream. Beyond doubt there is a
fairy procession marching along those frail
arcades and translucent corridors.

> " Their oaten pipes blow wondrous shrill,
>   The hemlock small blow clear."

And hark ! is that the ringing of Titania's
bridle, or the bells of the wee, wee hawk
that sits on Oberon's wrist ? This wonder
of Frost's handiwork may be had every winter, but he can do better than this, though
I have seen it but once in my life. There
had been a thaw without wind or rain, making the air fat with gray vapor. Towards
sundown came that chill, the avant-courier
of a northwesterly gale. Then, though there

was no perceptible current in the atmosphere, the fog began to attach itself in frosty
roots and filaments to the southern side of
every twig and grass-stem. The very posts
had poems traced upon them by this dumb
minstrel. Wherever the moist seeds found
lodgment grew an inch-deep moss fine as
cobweb, a slender coral-reef, argentine, delicate, as of some silent sea in the moon, such
as Agassiz dredges when he dreams. The
frost, too, can wield a delicate graver, and
in fancy leaves Piranesi far behind. He
covers your window-pane with Alpine etch-
ings, as if in memory of that sanctuary where
he finds shelter even in midsummer.

Now look down from your hillside across
the valley. The trees are leafless, but this
is the season to study their anatomy, and did
you ever notice before how much color there
is in the twigs of many of them? And the
smoke from those chimneys is so blue it
seems like a feeder of the sky into which it
flows. Winter refines it and gives it agreeable associations. In summer it suggests
cookery or the drudgery of steam-engines,

but now your fancy (if it can forget for
a moment the dreary usurpation of stoves)
traces it down to the fireside and the brightened faces of children. Thoreau is the only
poet who has fitly sung it. The wood-cutter
rises before day and

" First in the dusky dawn he sends abroad
  His early scout, his emissary, smoke,
  The earliest, latest pilgrim from his roof,
  To feel the frosty air ; . . . .
  And, while he crouches still beside the hearth,
  Nor musters courage to unbar the door,
  It has gone down the glen with the light wind
  And o'er the plain unfurled its venturous wreath,
  Draped the tree-tops, loitered upon the hill,
  And warmed the pinions of the early bird ;
  And now, perchance, high in the crispy air,
  Has caught sight of the day o'er the earth's edge,
  And greets its master's eye at his low door
  As some refulgent cloud in the upper sky."

Here is very bad verse and very good
imagination. He had been reading Wordsworth, or he would not have made *tree-tops*
an iambus. In the *Moretum* of Virgil (or,
if not his, better than most of his) is a pretty
picture of a peasant kindling his winter-
morning fire. He rises before dawn,

Sollicitaque manu tenebras explorat inertes
Vestigatque focum læsus quem denique sensit.
Parvulus exusto remanebat stipite fumus,
Et cinis obductæ celabat lumina prunæ.
Admovet his pronam submissa fronte lucernam,
Et producit acu stupas humore carentes,
Excitat et crebris languentem flatibus ignem ;
Tandem concepto tenebræ fulgore recedunt,
Oppositaque manu lumen defendit ab aura.

With cautious hand he gropes the sluggish dark,
Tracking the hearth which, scorched, he feels erelong.
In burnt-out logs a slender smoke remained,
And raked-up ashes hid the cinders' eyes ;
Stooping, to these the lamp outstretched he nears,
And, with a needle loosening the dry wick,
With frequent breath excites the languid flame.
Before the gathering glow the shades recede,
And his bent hand the new-caught light defends.

Ovid heightens the picture by a single
touch : —

Ipse genu poito flammas exsuscitat aura.

Kneeling, his breath calls back to life the flames.

If you walk down now into the woods,
you may find a robin or a bluebird among
the red-cedars, or a nuthatch scaling devi-

ously the trunk of some hardwood tree with
an eye as keen as that of a French soldier
foraging for the *pot-au-feu* of his mess.
Perhaps a blue-jay shrills *cah cah* in his
corvine trebles, or a chickadee

> "Shows feats of his gymnastic play,
> Head downward, clinging to the spray."

But both him and the snow-bird I love
better to see, tiny fluffs of feathered life, as
they scurry about in a driving mist of snow,
than in this serene air.

Coleridge has put into verse one of the
most beautiful phenomena of a winter
walk : —

> "The woodman winding westward up the glen
> At wintry dawn, where o'er the sheep-track's maze
> The viewless snow-mist weaves a glistening haze,
> Sees full before him, gliding without tread,
> An image with a halo round its head."

But this aureole is not peculiar to winter.
I have noticed it often in a summer morning, when the grass was heavy with dew,
and even later in the day, when the dewless

grass was still fresh enough to have a gleam
of its own.

For my own part I prefer a winter walk
that take in the nightfall and the intense
silence that erelong follows it.   The evening
lamps look yellower by contrast with the
snow, and give the windows that hearty
look of which our secretive fires have almost
robbed them.   The stars seem

> "To hang, like twinkling winter lamps,
>   Among the branches of the leafless trees,"

or, if you are on a hill-top (whence it is
sweet to watch the home-lights gleam out
one by one), they look nearer than in
summer, and appear to take a conscious part
in the cold.   Especially in one of those
stand-stills of the air that forebode a change
of weather, the sky is dusted with motes of
fire of which the summer-watcher never
dreamed.   Winter, too, is, on the whole, the
triumphant season of the moon, a moon
devoid of sentiment, if you choose, but
with the refreshment of a purer intellectual
light, — the cooler orb of middle life.   Who

ever saw anything to match that gleam,
rather divined than seen, which runs before
her over the snow, a breath of light, as she
rises on the infinite silence of winter night?
High in the heavens, also she seems to bring
out some intenser property of cold with her
chilly polish. The poets have instinctively
noted this. When Goody Blake imprecates
a curse of perpetual chill upon Harry Gill,
she has

> "The cold, cold moon above her head";

and Coleridge speaks of

> "The silent icicles,
> Quietly gleaming to the quiet moon."

As you walk homeward, — for it is time
that we should end our ramble, — you may
perchance hear the most impressive sound
in nature, unless it be the fall of a tree in
the forest during the hush of summer noon.
It is the stifled shriek of the lake yonder
as the frost throttles it. Wordsworth has
described it (too much, I fear, in the style
of Dr. Armstrong) : —

"And, interrupting oft that eager game,
  From under Esthwaite's splitting fields of ice,
  The pent-up air, struggling to free itself,
  Gave out to meadow-grounds and hills a loud
  Protracted yelling, like the noise of wolves
  Howling in troops along the Bothnic main."

Thoreau (unless the English lakes have a
different dialect from ours) calls it admirably
well a " whoop."   But it is a noise like none
other, as if Demogorgon were moaning in-
articulately from under the earth.   Let us
get within doors, lest we hear it again, for
there is something bodeful and uncanny
in it.

" Presently our hunter came back."

A MOOSEHEAD JOURNAL.

CONTENTS.

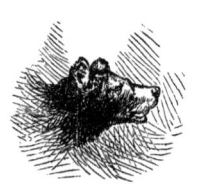

ILLUSTRATIONS.

A MOOSEHEAD JOURNAL.

Addressed to the Edelmann Storg at the Bagni di
Lucca.

HURSDAY, 11*th* *August.* — I knew
as little yesterday of the interior of
Maine as the least penetrating person
knows of the inside of that great social mill-
stone which, driven by the river Time, sets
imperatively agoing the several wheels of our
individual activities. Born while Maine was
still a province of native Massachusetts, I was
as much a foreigner to it as yourself, my dear
Storg. I had seen many lakes, ranging from
that of Virgil's Cumæan to that of Scott's
Caledonian Lady ; but Moosehead, within two
days of me, had never enjoyed the profit of
being mirrored in my retina. At the sound of
the name, no reminiscential atoms (according

to Kenelm Digby's Theory of Association, —
as good as any) stirred and marshalled themselves in my brain. The truth is, we think
lightly of Nature's penny shows, and estimate
what we see by the cost of the ticket. Em-
pedocles gave his life for a pit-entrance to
Ætna, and no doubt found his account in it.
Accordingly, the clean face of Cousin Bull is
imaged patronizingly in Lake George, and
Loch Lomond glasses the hurried countenance
of Jonathan, diving deeper in the streams of
European association (and coming up drier)
than any other man. Or is the cause of our
not caring to see what is equally within the
reach of all our neighbors to be sought in that
aristocratic principle so deeply implanted in
human nature ? I knew a pauper graduate
who always borrowed a black coat, and came
to eat the Commencement dinner, — not that
it was better than the one which daily graced
the board of the public institution in which he
hibernated (so to speak) during the other three
hundred and sixty-four days of the year, save
in this one particular, that none of his eleemosynary fellow-commoners could eat it. If

there are unhappy men who wish that they
were as the Babe Unborn, there are more who
would aspire to the lonely distinction of being
that other figurative personage, the Oldest
Inhabitant.   You remember the charming ir-
resolution of our dear Esthwaite, (like Mac-
heath between his two doxies,) divided between
his theory that he is under thirty, and his pride
at being the only one of us who witnessed the
September gale and the rejoicings at the Peace ?
Nineteen years ago I was walking through the
Franconia Notch, and stopped to chat with a
hermit, who fed with gradual logs the un-
wearied teeth of a saw-mill.   As the panting
steel slit off the *slabs* of the log, so did the less
willing machine of talk, acquiring a steadier
up-and-down motion, pare away that outward
bark of conversation which protects the core,
and which, like other bark, has naturally most
to do with the weather, the season, and the
heat of the day.   At length I asked him the
best point of view for the Old Man of the
Mountain.

"Dunno, — never see it."

Too young and too happy either to feel or

affect the Juvenalian indifference, I was sincerely astonished, and I expressed it.

The log-compelling man attempted no justification, but after a little asked, " Come from Bawsn ? "

" Yes " (with peninsular pride).

" Goodle to see in the vycinity o' Bawsn."

" O yes ! " I said, and I thought, — see Boston and die ! see the State Houses, old and new, the caterpillar wooden bridges crawling with innumerable legs across the flats of Charles ; see the Common, — largest park, doubtless, in the world, — with its files of trees planted as if by a drill-sergeant, and then for your *nunc dimittis !*

" I should like, 'awl, I *should* like to stan, on Bunker Hill. You 've ben there offen, likely ? "

" N—o—o," unwillingly, seeing the little end of the horn in clear vision at the terminus of this Socratic perspective.

" 'Awl, my young frien', you 've larned neow thet wut a man *kin* see any day for nawthin', childern half price, he never doos see. Nawthin' pay, nawthin' vally."

With this modern instance of a wise saw, I departed, deeply revolving these things with myself, and convinced that, whatever the ratio of population, the average amount of human nature to the square mile is the same the world over. I thought of it when I saw people upon the Pincian wondering at the Alchemist sun, as if he never burned the leaden clouds to gold in sight of Charles Street. I thought of it when I found eyes first discovering at Mont Blanc how beautiful snow was. As I walked on, I said to myself, There is one exception, wise hermit, — it is just these *gratis* pictures which the poet puts in his show-box, and which we all gladly pay Wordsworth and the rest for a peep at. The divine faculty is to see what everybody can look at.

While every well-informed man in Europe, from the barber down to the diplomatist, has his view of the Eastern Question, why should I not go personally down East and see for myself? Why not, like Tancred, attempt my own solution of the Mystery of the Orient, — doubly mysterious when you begin the two words with capitals? You know my way of

doing things, to let them simmer in my mind
gently for months, and at last do them *im-
promptu* in a kind of desperation, driven by the
Eumenides of unfulfilled purpose. So, after
talking about Moosehead till nobody believed
me capable of going thither, I found myself at
the Eastern Railway station. The only event
of the journey hither (I am now at Waterville)
was a boy hawking exhilaratingly the last great
railroad smash, — thirteen lives lost, — and no
doubt devoutly wishing there had been fifty.
This having a mercantile interest in horrors,
holding stock, as it were, in murder, misfortune,
and pestilence, must have an odd effect on the
human mind. The birds of ill-omen, at whose
sombre flight the rest of the world turn pale,
are the ravens which bring food to this little
outcast in the wilderness. If this lad give
thanks for daily bread, it would be curious to
inquire what that phrase represents to his un-
derstanding. If there ever be a plum in it, it
is Sin or Death that puts it in. Other details
of my dreadful ride I will spare you. Suffice
it that I arrived here in safety, — in complexion
like an Ethiopian serenader half got-up, and so

broiled and peppered that I was more like a devilled kidney than anything else I can think of.

10 P. M. — The civil landlord and neat chamber at the " Elmwood House " were very grateful, and after tea I set forth to explore the town. It has a good chance of being pretty; but, like most American towns, it is in a hobbledehoy age, growing yet, and one cannot tell what may happen. A child with great promise of beauty is often spoiled by its second teeth. There is something agreeable in the sense of completeness which a walled town gives one. It is entire, like a crystal, — a work which man has succeeded in finishing. I think the human mind pines more or less where everything is new, and is better for a diet of stale bread. The number of Americans who visit the Old World is beginning to afford matter of speculation to observant Europeans, and the deep inspirations with which they breathe the air of antiquity, as if their mental lungs had been starved with too thin an atmosphere. For my own part, I never saw a house which I thought old enough to be torn down. It is too like that Scythian fashion of knocking old

people on the head. I cannot help thinking that the indefinable something which we call *character* is cumulative, — that the influence of the same climate, scenery, and associations for several generations is necessary to its gathering head, and that the process is disturbed by continual change of place. The American is nomadic in religion, in ideas, in morals, and leaves his faith and opinions with as much indifference as the house in which he was born. However, we need not bother : Nature takes care not to leave out of the great heart of society either of its two ventricles of hold-back and go-ahead.

It seems as if every considerable American town must have its one specimen of everything, and so there is a college in Waterville, the buildings of which are three in number, of brick, and quite up to the average ugliness which seems essential in edifices of this description. Unhappily, they do not reach that extreme of ugliness where it and beauty come together in the clasp of fascination. We erect handsomer factories for cottons, woollens, and steam-engines, than for doctors, lawyers, and

parsons. The truth is, that, till our struggle
with nature is over, till this shaggy hemi-
sphere is tamed and subjugated, the workshop
will be the college whose degrees will be most
valued. Moreover, steam has made travel so
easy that the great university of the world is
open to all comers, and the old cloister system is falling astern. Perhaps it is only the
more needed, and, were I rich, I should like
to found a few lazyships in my Alma Mater
as a kind of counterpoise. The Anglo-Saxon
race has accepted the primal curse as a blessing, has deified work, and would not have
thanked Adam for abstaining from the apple.
They would have dammed the four rivers
of Paradise, substituted cotton for fig-leaves
among the antediluvian populations, and com-
mended man's first disobedience as a wise
measure of political economy. But to return
to our college. We cannot have fine buildings till we are less in a hurry. We snatch
an education like a meal at a railroad-station.
Just in time to make us dyspeptic, the whistle
shrieks, and we must rush, or lose our places
in the great train of life. Yet noble architec-

ture is one element of patriotism, and an eminent one of culture, the finer portions of which are taken in by unconscious absorption through the pores of the mind from the surrounding atmosphere. I suppose we must wait, for we are a great bivouac as yet rather than a nation, — on the march from the Atlantic to the Pacific, — and pitch tents instead of building houses. Our very villages seem to be in motion, following westward the bewitching music of some Pied Piper of Hamelin. We still feel the great push toward sundown given to the peoples somewhere in the gray dawn of history. The cliff-swallow alone of all animated nature emigrates eastward.

Friday, 12th. — The coach leaves Waterville at five o'clock in the morning, and one must breakfast in the dark at a quarter past four, because a train starts at twenty minutes before five, — the passengers by both conveyances being pastured gregariously. So one must be up at half past three. The primary geological formations contain no trace of man, and it seems to me that these eocene periods of the day are not fitted for sustaining the human forms of life. One of the Fathers held that the sun was created to be worshipped at his rising by the Gentiles. The more reason that Christians (except, perhaps, early Christians) should abstain from these heathenish ceremonials. As one arriving by an early train is welcomed by a drowsy maid with the sleep scarce brushed out of her hair, and finds empty grates and polished mahogany, on whose arid plains the pioneers of breakfast have not yet encamped, so a person waked thus unseasonably is sent into the world before his faculties are up and dressed to serve him. It might have been for this reason that my stomach resented for several hours a piece of fried beefsteak which I forced upon it, or, more properly speaking, a piece of that leathern conveniency which in these regions assumes the name. You will find it as hard to believe, my dear Storg, as that quarrel of the Sorbonists, whether one should say *ego amat* or no, that the use of the gridiron is unknown hereabout, and so near a river named after St. Lawrence, too!

To-day has been the hottest day of the sea-

son, yet our drive has not been unpleasant.
For a considerable distance we followed the
course of the Sebasticook River, a pretty
stream with alternations of dark brown pools
and wine-colored rapids. On each side of the
road the land had been cleared, and little one-
story farm-houses were scattered at intervals.
But the stumps still held out in most of the
fields, and the tangled wilderness closed in
behind, striped here and there with the slim
white trunks of the elm. As yet only the
edges of the great forest have been nibbled
away. Sometimes a root-fence stretched up
its bleaching antlers, like the trophies of a
giant hunter. Now and then the houses
thickened into an unsocial-looking village, and
we drove up to the grocery to leave and take
a mail-bag, stopping again presently to water
the horses at some pallid little tavern, whose
one red-curtained eye (the bar-room) had been
put out by the inexorable thrust of Maine
Law. Had Shenstone travelled this road, he
would never have written that famous stanza
of his; had Johnson, he would never have
quoted it. They are to real inns as the skull

of Yorick to his face. Where these villages
occurred at a distance from the river, it was
difficult to account for them. On the river-
bank, a saw-mill or a tannery served as a logi-
cal premise, and saved them from total incon-
sequentiality. As we trailed along, at the
rate of about four miles an hour, it was discovered that one of our mail-bags was missing.
"Guess somebody'll pick it up," said the
driver coolly: "'t any rate, likely there's
nothin' in it." Who knows how long it took
some Elam D. or Zebulon K. to compose the
missive intrusted to that vagrant bag, and
how much longer to persuade Pamela Grace
or Sophronia Melissa that it had really and
truly been written? The discovery of our
loss was made by a tall man who sat next to
me on the top of the coach, every one of
whose senses seemed to be prosecuting its
several investigation as we went along. Presently, sniffing gently, he remarked: "'Pears
to me 's though I smelt sunthin'. Ain't the
aix het, think?" The driver pulled up, and,
sure enough, the off fore-wheel was found
to be smoking. In three minutes he had

snatched a rail from the fence, made a lever,
raised the coach, and taken off the wheel,
bathing the hot axle and box with water from
the river. It was a pretty spot, and I was
not sorry to lie under a beech-tree (Tityrus-
like, meditating over my pipe) and watch the
operations of the fire-annihilator. I could not
help contrasting the ready helpfulness of our
driver, all of whose wits were about him, current, and redeemable in the specie of action on
emergency, with an incident of travel in Italy,
where, under a somewhat similar stress of cir-
cumstances, our *vetturino* had nothing for it
but to dash his hat on the ground and call on
Sant' Antonio, the Italian Hercules.

There being four passengers for the Lake,
a vehicle called a mud-wagon was detailed
at Newport for our accommodation. In this
we jolted and rattled along at a livelier pace
than in the coach. As we got farther north,
the country (especially the hills) gave evi-
dence of longer cultivation. About the thriv-
ing town of Dexter we saw fine farms and
crops. The houses, too, became prettier;
hop-vines were trained about the doors, and

hung their clustering thyrsi over the open
windows. A kind of wild rose (called by
the country folk the primrose) and asters were
planted about the door-yards, and orchards,
commonly of natural fruit, added to the pleasant home-look. But everywhere we could
see that the war between the white man and
the forest was still fierce, and that it would
be a long while yet before the axe was buried.
The haying being over, fires blazed or smoul-
dered against the stumps in the fields, and the
blue smoke widened slowly upward through
the quiet August atmosphere. It seemed to
me that I could hear a sigh now and then
from the immemorial pines, as they stood
watching these camp-fires of the inexorable
invader. Evening set in, and, as we crunched
and crawled up the long gravelly hills, I sometimes began to fancy that Nature had forgot-
ten to make the corresponding descent on
the other side. But erelong we were rushing
down at full speed; and, inspired by the
dactylic beat of the horses' hoofs, I essayed
to repeat the opening lines of Evangeline.
At the moment I was beginning, we plunged

into a hollow, where the soft clay had been
overcome by a road of unhewn logs. I got
through one line to this corduroy accompani-
ment, somewhat as a country choir stretches
a short metre on the Procrustean rack of a long-
drawn tune. The result was like this : —

" Thihis ihis thehe fohorest prihihimeheval ; thehe
   murhurmuring pihines hahand thehe hehem-
   lohocks ! "

At a quarter past eleven, P. M., we reached
Greenville, (a little village which looks as if it
had dripped down from the hills, and settled
in the hollow at the foot of the lake,) having
accomplished seventy-two miles in eighteen
hours. The tavern was totally extinguished.
The driver rapped upon the bar-room window,
and after a while we saw heat-lightnings of unsuccessful matches followed by a low grumble
of vocal thunder, which I am afraid took the
form of imprecation. Presently there was a
great success, and the steady blur of lighted
tallow succeeded the fugitive brilliance of the
pine. A hostler fumbled the door open, and
stood staring at but not seeing us, with the

sleep sticking out all over him. We at last
contrived to launch him, more like an insensi-
ble missile than an intelligent or intelligible
being, at the slumbering landlord, who came
out wide-awake, and welcomed us as so many
half-dollars, — twenty-five cents each for bed,
ditto breakfast. O Shenstone, Shenstone !
The only roost was in the garret, which had
been made into a single room, and contained
eleven double-beds, ranged along the walls.
It was like sleeping in a hospital. However,
nice customs curtsy to eighteen-hour rides, and
we slept.

Saturday, 13*th*. — This morning I performed
my toilet in the bar-room, where there was an
abundant supply of water, and a halo of interested spectators. After a sufficient breakfast,
we embarked on the little steamer Moosehead,
and were soon throbbing up the lake. The
boat, it appeared, had been chartered by a
party, this not being one of her regular trips.
Accordingly we were mulcted in twice the
usual fee, the philosophy of which I could not
understand. However, it always comes easier
to us to comprehend why we receive than why

we pay. I dare say it was quite clear to the captain. There were three or four clearings on the western shore; but after passing these, the lake became wholly primeval, and looked to us as it did to the first adventurous French- man who paddled across it. Sometimes a cleared point would be pink with the blossom- ing willow-herb, " a cheap and excellent sub- stitute " for heather, and, like all such, not *quite* so good as the real thing. On all sides rose deep-blue mountains of remarkably grace- ful outline, and more fortunate than common in their names. There were the Big and Little Squaw, the Spencer and Lily-bay Mountains. It was debated whether we saw Katahdin or not (perhaps more useful as an intellectual exercise than the assured vision would have been), and presently Mount Kineo rose ab- ruptly before us, in shape not unlike the island of Capri. Mountains are called great natural features, and why they should not retain their names long enough for them also to become naturalized, it is hard to say. Why should every new surveyor rechristen them with the gubernatorial patronymics of the current year?

They are geological noses, and, as they are
aquiline or pug, indicate terrestrial idiosyn-
crasies. A cosmical physiognomist, after a
glance at them, will draw no vague inference
as to the character of the country. The word
nose is no better than any other word; but
since the organ has got that name, it is convenient to keep it. Suppose we had to label
our facial prominences every season with the
name of our provincial governor, how should
we like it? If the old names have no other
meaning, they have that of age; and, after all,
meaning is a plant of slow growth, as every
reader of Shakespeare knows. It is well
enough to call mountains after their discoverers, for Nature has a knack of throwing doub-
lets, and somehow contrives it that discoverers
have good names. Pike's Peak is a curious
hit in this way. But these surveyors' names
have no natural *stick* in them. They remind
one of the epithets of poetasters, which peel off
like a badly gummed postage-stamp. The
early settlers did better, and there is something pleasant in the sound of Graylock, Sad-
dleback, and Great Haystack.

> " I love those names
> Wherewith the exiled farmer tames
> Nature down to companionship
>   With his old world's more homely mood,
> And strives the shaggy wild to clip
>   With arms of familiar habitude."

It is possible that Mount Marcy and Mount Hitchcock may sound as well hereafter as Hellespont and Peloponnesus, when the heroes, their namesakes, have become mythic with antiquity. But that is to look forward a great way. I am no fanatic for Indian nomenclature, — the name of my native district having been Pigsgusset, — but let us at least agree on names for ten years.

There were a couple of loggers on board, in red flannel shirts, and with rifles. They were the first I had seen, and I was interested in their appearance. They were tall, well-knit men, straight as Robin Hood, and with a quiet, self-contained look that pleased me. I fell into talk with one of them.

" Is there a good market for the farmers here in the woods ? " I asked.

" None better. They can sell what they

raise at their doors, and for the best of prices.
The lumberers want it all, and more."

"It must be a lonely life. But then we all
have to pay more or less life for a living."

"Well, it *is* lonesome. Should n't like it.
After all, the best crop a man can raise is a
good crop of society. We don't live none too
long, anyhow ; and without society a fellow
could n't tell mor 'n half the time whether he
was alive or not."

This speech gave me a glimpse into the life
of the lumberers' camp. It was plain that
there a man would soon find out how much
alive he was, — there he could learn to estimate his quality, weighed in the nicest self-
adjusting balance. The best arm at the axe
or the paddle, the surest eye for a road or for
the weak point of a *jam*, the steadiest foot upon
the squirming log, the most persuasive voice
to the tugging oxen, — all these things are
rapidly settled, and so an aristocracy is evolved
from this democracy of the woods, for good
old mother Nature speaks Saxon still, and
with her either Canning or Kenning means
King.

A string of five loons was flying back and
forth in long, irregular zigzags, uttering at
intervals their wild, tremulous cry, which always seems far away, like the last faint pulse
of echo dying among the hills, and which is
one of those few sounds that, instead of dis-
turbing solitude, only deepen and confirm it.
On our inland ponds they are usually seen in
pairs, and I asked if it were common to meet
five together. My question was answered by
a queer-looking old man, chiefly remarkable for
a pair of enormous cowhide boots, over which
large blue trousers of frocking strove in vain
to crowd themselves.

"Wahl, 't ain't ushil," said he, "and it's
called a sign o' rain comin', that is."

"Do you think it will rain?"

With the caution of a veteran *auspex*, he
evaded a direct reply. "Wahl, they *du* say
it's a sign o' rain comin'," said he.

I discovered afterward that my interlocutor
was Uncle Zeb. Formerly, every New England town had its representative uncle. He
was not a pawnbroker, but some elderly man
who, for want of more defined family ties, had

"' Wahl, 't ain't ushil,' said he."

gradually assumed this avuncular relation to
the community, inhabiting the border-land between respectability and the almshouse, with
no regular calling, but working at haying, wood-
sawing, whitewashing, associated with the de-
mise of pigs and the ailments of cattle, and
possessing as much patriotism as might be im-
plied in a devoted attachment to "New England" — with a good deal of sugar and very
little water in it. Uncle Zeb was a good
specimen of this palæozoic class, extinct among
us for the most part, or surviving, like the
Dodo, in the Botany Bays of society. He was
ready to contribute (somewhat muddily) to all
general conversation; but his chief topics
were his boots and the 'Roostick war. Upon
the lowlands and levels of ordinary palaver he
would make rapid and unlooked-for incursions;
but, provision failing, he would retreat to these
two fastnesses, whence it was impossible to
dislodge him, and to which he knew innumerable passes and short cuts quite beyond the
conjecture of common woodcraft. His mind
opened naturally to these two subjects, like a
book to some favorite passage. As the ear ac-

customs itself to any sound recurring regularly, such as the ticking of a clock, and, without a conscious effort of attention, takes no impression from it whatever, so does the mind find a natural safeguard against this pendulum species of discourse, and performs its duties in the parliament by an unconscious reflex action, like the beating of the heart or the movement of the lungs. If talk seemed to be flagging, our Uncle would put the heel of one boot upon the toe of the other, to bring it within point-blank range, and say, " Wahl, I stump the Devil himself to make that 'ere boot hurt *my* foot," leaving us in doubt whether it were the virtue of the foot or its case which set at nought the wiles of the adversary ; or, looking up suddenly, he would exclaim, " Wahl, we eat *some* beans to the 'Roostick war, I tell *you !* " When his poor old clay was wet with gin, his thoughts and words acquired a rank flavor from it, as from too strong a fertilizer. At such times, too, his fancy commonly reverted to a pre-historic period of his life, when he singly had settled all the surrounding country, subdued the Injuns and other wild animals, and named all the towns.

We talked of the winter-camps and the life there. " The best thing is," said our uncle, " to hear a log squeal thru the snow. Git a good, cole, frosty mornin', in Febuary say, an' take an' hitch the critters on to a log that 'll scale seven thousan', an' it 'll squeal as pooty as an'thin' *you* ever hearn, I tell *you*."

A pause.

" Lessee, — seen Cal Hutchins lately ? "

" No."

" Seems to me 's though I hed n't seen Cal sence the 'Roostick war. Wahl," etc., etc.

Another pause.

" To look at them boots you 'd think they was too large; but kind o' git your foot into 'em, and they 're as easy 's a glove." (I observed that he never seemed really to get his foot in, — there was always a qualifying *kind o'*.) " Wahl, my foot can play in 'em like a young hedgehog."

By this time we had arrived at Kineo, — a flourishing village of one house, the tavern kept by 'Squire Barrows. The 'Squire is a large, hearty man, with a voice as clear and strong as a northwest wind, and a great laugh

suitable to it.   His table is neat and well supplied, and he waits upon it himself in the good
old landlordly fashion.   One may be much
better off here, to my thinking, than in one of
those gigantic Columbaria which are foisted
upon us patient Americans for hotels, and
where one is packed away in a pigeon-hole so
near the heavens that, if the comet should flirt
its tail, (no unlikely thing in the month of flies,)
one would be in danger of being brushed
away.   Here one does not pay his diurnal
three dollars for an undivided five-hundredth
part of the pleasure of looking at gilt gingerbread.   Here one's relations are with the monarch himself, and one is not obliged to wait
the slow leisure of those "attentive clerks"
whose praises are sung by thankful deadheads,
and to whom the slave who pays may feel as
much gratitude as might thrill the heart of a
brown-paper parcel toward the express-man
who labels it and chucks it under his counter.

Sunday, 14th. — The loons were right.
About midnight it began to rain in earnest,
and did not hold up till about ten o'clock this
morning.   "This is a Maine dew," said a

shaggy woodman cheerily, as he shook the water out of his wide-awake, " if it don't look out
sharp, it 'll begin to rain afore it thinks on 't."
The day was mostly spent within doors; but
I found good and intelligent society. We
should have to be shipwrecked on Juan Fer-
nandez not to find men who knew more than
we. In these travelling encounters one is
thrown upon his own resources, and is worth
just what he carries about him. The social
currency of home, the smooth-worn coin which
passes freely among friends and neighbors, is
of no account. We are thrown back upon the
old system of barter; and, even with savages,
we bring away only as much of the wild wealth
of the woods as we carry beads of thought and
experience, strung one by one in painful years,
to pay for them with. A useful old jackknife
will buy more than the daintiest Louis Quinze
paper-folder fresh from Paris. Perhaps the
kind of intelligence one gets in these out-of-the-
way places is the best, — where one takes a
fresh man after breakfast instead of the damp
morning paper, and where the magnetic telegraph of human sympathy flashes swift news
from brain to brain.

Meanwhile, at a pinch, to-morrow's weather
can be discussed. The augury from the flight
of birds is favorable, — the loons no longer
prophesying rain. The wind also is hauling
round to the right quarter, according to some,
to the wrong, if we are to believe others.
Each man has his private barometer of hope,
the mercury in which is more or less sensitive,
and the opinion vibrant with its rise or fall.
Mine has an index which can be moved me-
chanically. I fixed it at *set fair*, and resigned
myself. I read an old volume of the Patent-
Office Report on Agriculture, and stored away
a beautiful pile of facts and observations for
future use, which the current of occupation,
at its first freshet, would sweep quietly off to
blank oblivion. Practical application is the
only mordant which will set things in the
memory. Study, without it, is gymnastics,
and not work, which alone will get intellectual
bread. One learns more metaphysics from a
single temptation than from all the philosophers. It is curious, though, how tyrannical
the habit of reading is, and what shifts we
make to escape thinking. There is no bore

we dread being left alone with so much as our
own minds. I have seen a sensible man study
a stale newspaper in a country tavern, and
husband it as he would an old shoe on a raft
after shipwreck. Why not try a bit of hiber-
nation? There are few brains that would not
be better for living on their own fat a little
while. * With these reflections, I, notwith-
standing, spent the afternoon over my Report.
If our own experience is of so little use to us,
what a dolt is he who recommends to man or
nation the experience of others! Like the
mantle in the old ballad, it is always too short
or too long, and exposes or trips us up. "Keep
out of that candle," says old Father Miller,
" or you 'll get a singeing." "Pooh, pooh,
father, I 've been dipped in the new asbestos
preparation," and *frozz !* it is all over with
young Hopeful. How many warnings have
been drawn from Pretorian bands, and Janiza-
ries, and Mamelukes, to make Napoleon III.
impossible in 1851 ! I found myself thinking
the same thoughts over again, when we walked
later on the beach and picked up pebbles.
The old time-ocean throws upon its shores

just such rounded and polished results of the
eternal turmoil, but we only see the beauty of
those we have got the headache in stooping
for ourselves, and wonder at the dull brown
bits of common stone with which our comrades
have stuffed their pockets. Afterwards this
little fable came of it.

DOCTOR LOBSTER.

A PERCH, who had the toothache, once
Thus moaned, like any human dunce:
" Why must great souls exhaust so soon
Life's thin and unsubstantial boon ?
Existence on such sculpin terms, —
Their vulgar loves and hard-won worms, —
What is it all but dross to me,
Whose nature craves a larger sea ;
Whose inches, six from head to tail,
Enclose the spirit of a whale;
Who, if great baits were still to win,
By watchful eye and fearless fin
Might with the Zodiac's awful twain
Room for a third immortal gain ?
Better the crowd's unthinking plan, —
The hook, the jerk, the frying-pan !
O Death, thou ever roaming shark,
Ingulf me in eternal dark ! "

The speech was cut in two by flight :
A real shark had come in sight ;
No metaphoric monster, one
It soothes despair to call upon,
But stealthy, sidelong, grim, I wis,
A bit of downright Nemesis ;
While it recovered from the shock,
Our fish took shelter 'neath a rock :
This was an ancient lobster's house,
A lobster of prodigious *nous*,
So old that barnacles had spread
Their white encampments o'er its head,
And of experience so stupend,
His claws were blunted at the end,
Turning life's iron pages o'er,
That shut and can be oped no more.

Stretching a hospitable claw,
" At once," said he, " the point I saw ;
My dear young friend, your case I rue,
Your great-great-grandfather I knew ;
He was a tried and tender friend
I know, — I ate him in the end :
In this vile sea a pilgrim long,
Still my sight 's good, my memory strong ;
The only sign that age is near
Is a slight deafness in this ear ;
I understand your case as well
As this my old familiar shell ;

This sorrow 's a new-fangled notion,
Come in since first I knew the ocean;
We had no radicals, nor crimes,
Nor lobster-pots, in good old times;
Your traps and nets and hooks we owe
To Messieurs Louis Blanc and Co.;
I say to all my sons and daughters,
Shun Red Republican hot waters;
No lobster ever cast his lot
Among the reds, but went to pot:
Your trouble 's in the jaw, you said?
Come, let me just nip off your head,
And, when a new one comes, the pain
Will never trouble you again:
Nay, nay, fear naught: 't is nature's law.
Four times I've lost this starboard claw;
And still, erelong, another grew,
Good as the old, — and better too!"

The perch consented, and next day
An osprey, marketing that way,
Picked up a fish without a head,
Floating with belly up, stone dead.

MORAL.

Sharp are the teeth of ancient saws,
And sauce for goose is gander's sauce;
But perch's heads are n't lobster's claws.

Monday, 15th. — The morning was fine,
and we were called at four o'clock. At the
moment my door was knocked at, I was
mounting a giraffe with that charming *nil ad-
mirari* which characterizes dreams, to visit
Prester John. *Rat-tat-tat-tat!* upon my door
and upon the horn gate of dreams also. I
remarked to my skowhegan (the Tâtar for
giraffe-driver) that I was quite sure the ani-
mal had the *raps*, a common disease among
them, for I heard a queer knocking noise inside him. It is the sound of his joints, O
Tambourgi! (an Oriental term of reverence,)
and proves him to be of the race of El Kei-
rat. *Rat-tat-tat-too!* and I lost my dinner at
the Prester's, embarking for a voyage to the
Northwest Carry instead. Never use the
word *canoe*, my dear Storg, if you wish to
retain your self-respect. *Birch* is the term
among us backwoodsmen. I never knew it
till yesterday; but, like a true philosopher, I
made it appear as if I had been intimate with
it from childhood. The rapidity with which
the human mind levels itself to the standard
around it gives us the most pertinent warning

as to the company we keep. It is as hard
for most characters to stay at their own average point in all companies, as for a thermometer to say 65° for twenty-four hours together.
I like this in our friend Johannes Taurus, that
he carries everywhere and maintains his in-
sular temperature, and will have everything
accommodate itself to that. Shall I confess
that this morning I would rather have broken
the moral law, than have endangered the equi-
poise of the birch by my awkwardness? that
I should have been prouder of a compliment
to my paddling, than to have had both my
guides suppose me the author of Hamlet?
Well, Cardinal Richelieu used to jump over
chairs.

We were to paddle about twenty miles; but
we made it rather more by crossing and re-
crossing the lake. Twice we landed, — once
at a camp, where we found the cook alone,
baking bread and gingerbread. Monsieur
Soyer would have been startled a little by this
shaggy professor, — this Pre-Raphaelite of
cookery. He represented the *salæratus* period
of the art, and his bread was of a brilliant yel-

low, like those cakes tinged with saffron, which
hold out so long against time and the flies in
little water-side shops of seaport towns, —
dingy extremities of trade fit to moulder on
Lethe wharf. His water was better, squeezed
out of ice-cold granite in the neighboring
mountains, and sent through subterranean
ducts to sparkle up by the door of the camp.

"There 's nothin' so sweet an' hulsome as
your *real* spring water," said Uncle Zeb, " git
it pure. But it 's dreffle hard to git it that
ain't got sunthin' the matter of it. Snow-
water 'll burn a man's inside out, — I larned
that to the 'Roostick war, — and the snow
lays terrible long on some o' thes'ere hills.
Me an' Eb Stiles was up old Ktahdn once jest
about this time o' year, an' we come acrost a
kind o' holler like, as full o' snow as your
stockin 's full o' your foot. *I* see it fust, an'
took an' rammed a settin'-pole; wahl, it was
all o' twenty foot into 't, an' could n't fin' no
bottom. I dunno as there 's snow-water
enough in this to do no hurt. I don't somehow seem to think that *real* spring-water 's so
plenty as it used to be." And Uncle Zeb, with

perhaps a little over-refinement of scrupulosity, applied his lips to the Ethiop ones of a bottle of raw gin, with a kiss that drew out its very soul, — a *basia* that Secundus might have sung. He must have been a wonderful judge of water, for he analyzed this, and detected its latent snow simply by his eye, and without the clumsy process of tasting. I could not help thinking that he had made the desert his dwelling-place chiefly in order to enjoy the ministrations of this one fair spirit unmolested.

We pushed on. Little islands loomed trembling between sky and water, like hanging gardens. Gradually the filmy trees defined themselves, the aerial enchantment lost its potency, and we came up with common prose islands that had so late been magical and poetic. The old story of the attained and unattained. About noon we reached the head of the lake, and took possession of a deserted *wongen*, in which to cook and eat our dinner. No Jew, I am sure, can have a more thorough dislike of salt pork than I have in a normal state, yet I had already eaten it raw with hard bread for lunch, and relished it keenly. We

"We sat round and ate thankfully."

soon had our tea-kettle over the fire, and before long the cover was chattering with the escaping steam, which had thus vainly begged of all men to be saddled and bridled, till James Watt one day happened to overhear it. One of our guides shot three Canada grouse, and these were turned slowly between the fire and a bit of salt pork, which dropped fatness upon them as it fried. Although *my* fingers were certainly not made before knives and forks, yet they served as a convenient substitute for those more ancient inventions. We sat round, Turk-fashion, and ate thankfully, while a party of aborigines of the Mosquito tribe, who had camped in the *wongen* before we arrived, dined upon us. I do not know what the British Protectorate of the Mosquitoes amounts to; but, as I squatted there at the mercy of these blood-thirsty savages, I no longer wondered that the classic Everett had been stung into a willingness for war on the question.

"This 'ere 'd be about a complete place for a camp, ef there was on'y a spring o' sweet water handy. Frizzled pork goes wal, don't it? Yes, an' sets wal, too," said Uncle Zeb,

and he again tilted his bottle, which rose
nearer and nearer to an angle of forty-five at
every gurgle. He then broached a curious
dietetic theory : " The reason we take salt
pork along is cos it packs handy : you git the
greatest amount o' board in the smallest compass, — let alone that it 's more nourishin'
than an'thin' else. It kind o' don't disgest
so quick, but stays by ye, anourishin' ye all
the while.

" A feller can live wal on frizzled pork an'
good spring-water, git it *good*. To the 'Roostick war we did n't ask for nothin' better, —
on'y beans." (*Tilt, tilt, gurgle, gurgle.*)
Then, with an apparent feeling of inconsis-
tency, " But then, come to git used to a particular *kind* o' spring-water, an' it makes a
feller hard to suit. Most all sorts o' water
taste kind o' *in*sipid away from home. Now,
I 've gut a spring to my place that 's as sweet
— wahl, it 's as sweet as maple sap. A feller
acts about water jest as he does about a pair
o' boots. It 's all on it in gittin' wonted.
Now, *them* boots," etc., etc. (*Gurgle, gurgle,
gurgle, smack !*)

All this while he was packing away the remains of the pork and hard bread in two large firkins. This accomplished, we re-embarked, our uncle on his way to the birch essaying a kind of song in four or five parts, of which the words were hilarious and the tune profoundly melancholy, and which was finished, and the rest of his voice apparently jerked out of him in one sharp falsetto note, by his tripping over the root of a tree. We paddled a short distance up a brook which came into the lake smoothly through a little meadow not far off. We soon reached the Northwest Carry, and our guide, pointing through the woods, said : " That 's the Cannydy road. You can travel that clearn to Kebeck, a hundred an' twenty mile," — a privilege of which I respectfully declined to avail myself. The offer, however, remains open to the public. The Carry is called two miles ; but this is the estimate of somebody who had nothing to lug. I had a headache and all my baggage, which, with a traveller's instinct, I had brought with me. (P. S. — I did not even take the keys out of my pocket,

and both my bags were wet through before
I came back.) *My* estimate of the distance
is eighteen thousand six hundred and seventy-
four miles and three quarters, — the fraction
being the part left to be travelled after one
of my companions most kindly insisted on
relieving me of my heaviest bag. I know
very well that the ancient Roman soldiers
used to carry sixty pounds' weight, and all
that; but I am not, and never shall be, an
ancient Roman soldier, — no, not even in the
miraculous Thundering Legion. Uncle Zeb
slung the two provender firkins across his
shoulder, and trudged along, grumbling that
"he never see sech a contrairy pair as them."
He had begun upon a second bottle of his
"particular kind o' spring-water," and, at
every rest, the gurgle of this peripatetic fountain might be heard, followed by a smack, a
fragment of mosaic song, or a confused clatter
with the cowhide boots, being an arbitrary
symbol, intended to represent the festive
dance. Christian's pack gave him not half
so much trouble as the firkins gave Uncle
Zeb. It grew harder and harder to sling

"He had begun on a second bottle."

them, and with every fresh gulp of the Bata-
vian elixir, they got heavier. Or rather, the
truth was, that his hat grew heavier, in which
he was carrying on an extensive manufac-
ture of bricks without straw. At last affairs
reached a crisis, and a particularly favorable
pitch offering, with a puddle at the foot of it,
even *the* boots afforded no sufficient ballast,
and away went our uncle, the satellite firkins
accompanying faithfully his headlong flight.
Did ever exiled monarch or disgraced minis-
ter find the cause of his fall in himself? Is
there not always a strawberry at the bottom
of our cup of life, on which we can lay all
the blame of our deviations from the straight
path? Till now Uncle Zeb had contrived to
give a gloss of volition to smaller stumblings
and gyrations, by exaggerating them into an
appearance of playful burlesque. But the
present case was beyond any such subterfuges.
He held a bed of justice where he sat, and
then arose slowly, with a stern determination
of vengeance stiffening every muscle of his
face. But what would he select as the culprit? " It 's that cussed firkin," he mumbled

to himself. "I never knowed a firkin cair on so, — no, not in the 'Roostehicick war. There, go long, will ye? and don't come back till you've larned how to walk with a genelman!" And, seizing the unhappy scapegoat by the bail, he hurled it into the forest. It is a curious circumstance, that it was not the firkin containing the bottle which was thus condemned to exile.

The end of the Carry was reached at last, and, as we drew near it, we heard a sound of shouting and laughter. It came from a party of men making hay of the wild grass in Seboomok meadows, which lie around Seboomok pond, into which the Carry empties itself. Their camp was near, and our two hunters set out for it, leaving us seated in the birch on the plashy border of the pond. The repose was perfect. Another heaven hallowed and deepened the polished lake, and through that nether world the fish-hawk's double floated with balanced wings, or, wheeling suddenly, flashed his whitened breast against the sun. As the clattering kingfisher flew unsteadily across, and seemed to push his heavy head

along with ever-renewing effort, a visionary
mate flitted from downward tree to tree below.
Some tall alders shaded us from the sun, in
whose yellow afternoon light the drowsy forest was steeped, giving out that wholesome
resinous perfume, almost the only warm odor
which it is refreshing to breathe. The tame
haycocks in the midst of the wildness gave one
a pleasant reminiscence of home, like hearing
one's native tongue in a strange country.

Presently our hunters came back, bringing
with them a tall, thin, active-looking man,
with black eyes, that glanced unconsciously
on all sides, like one of those spots of sunlight
which a child dances up and down the street
with a bit of looking-glass. This was M., the
captain of the hay-makers, a famous river-
driver, and who was to have fifty men under
him next winter. I could now understand
that sleepless vigilance of eye. He had consented to take two of our party in his birch to
search for moose. A quick, nervous, decided
man, he got them into the birch, and was off
instantly, without a superfluous word. He evidently looked upon them as he would upon a

couple of logs which he was to deliver at a
certain place. Indeed, I doubt if life and the
world presented themselves to Napier himself
in a more logarithmic way. His only thought
was to do the immediate duty well, and to pilot
his particular raft down the crooked stream of
life to the ocean beyond. The birch seemed to
feel him as an inspiring soul, and slid away
straight and swift for the outlet of the pond.
As he disappeared under the overarching alders
of the brook, our two hunters could not re-
press a grave and measured applause. There
is never any extravagance among these woodmen; their eye, accustomed to reckoning the
number of feet which a tree will *scale*, is rapid
and close in its guess of the amount of stuff in
a man. It was *laudari a laudato*, however,
for they themselves were accounted good men
in a birch. I was amused, in talking with
them about him, to meet with an instance of
that tendency of the human mind to assign
some utterly improbable reason for gifts which
seem unaccountable. After due praise, one of
them said, " I guess he 's got some Injun in
him," although I knew very well that the

speaker had a thorough contempt for the
red-man, mentally and physically. Here was
mythology in a small way, — the same that
under more favorable auspices hatched Helen
out of an egg and gave Merlin an Incubus for
a father. I was pleased with all I saw of
M. He was in his narrow sphere a true ἄναξ
ἀνδρῶν, and the ragged edges of his old hat
seemed to become coronated as I looked at
him. He impressed me as a man really edu-
cated, — that is, with his aptitudes *drawn out*
and ready for use. He was A. M. and LL. D.
in Woods College, — Axe-master and Doctor
of Logs. Are not *our* educations commonly
like a pile of books laid over a plant in a pot ?
The compressed nature struggles through at
every crevice, but can never get the cramp
and stunt out of it. We spend all our youth
in building a vessel for our voyage of life, and
set forth with streamers flying; but the moment we come nigh the great loadstone mountain of our proper destiny, out leap all our
carefully-driven bolts and nails, and we get
many a mouthful of good salt brine, and many
a buffet of the rough water of experience, before we secure the bare right to live.

We now entered the outlet, a long-drawn
aisle of alder, on each side of which spired tall
firs, spruces, and white cedars. The motion
of the birch reminded me of the gondola, and
they represent among water-craft the *felidæ*,
the cat-tribe, stealthy, silent, treacherous, and
preying by night. I closed my eyes, and
strove to fancy myself in the dumb city, whose
only horses are the bronze ones of St. Mark.
But Nature would allow no rival, and bent
down an alder-bough to brush my cheek and
recall me. Only the robin sings in the emerald
chambers of these tall sylvan palaces, and the
squirrel leaps from hanging balcony to balcony.

The rain which the loons foreboded had
raised the west branch of the Penobscot so
much, that a strong current was setting back
into the pond ; and, when at last we brushed
through into the river, it was full to the brim,
— too full for moose, the hunters said. Rivers
with low banks have always the compensation
of giving a sense of entire fulness. The sun
sank behind its horizon of pines, whose pointed
summits notched the rosy west in an endless
black *sierra*. At the same moment the golden

moon swung slowly up in the east, like the other scale of that Homeric balance in which Zeus weighed the deeds of men. Sunset and moonrise at once! Adam had no more in Eden — except the head of Eve upon his shoulder. The stream was so smooth, that the floating logs we met seemed to hang in a glowing atmosphere, the shadow-half being as real as the solid. And gradually the mind was etherized to a like dreamy placidity, till fact and fancy, the substance and the image, floating on the current of reverie, became but as the upper and under halves of one unreal reality.

In the west still lingered a pale-green light. I do not know whether it be from greater familiarity, but it always seems to me that the pinnacles of pine-trees make an edge to the landscape which tells better against the twilight, or the fainter dawn before the rising moon, than the rounded and cloud-cumulus outline of hard-wood trees.

After paddling a couple of miles, we found the arbored mouth of the little Malahoodus River, famous for moose. We had been on

the look-out for it, and I was amused to hear
one of the hunters say to the other, to assure
himself of his familiarity with the spot, " You
drove the West Branch last spring, did n't
you ? " as one of us might ask about a horse.
We did not explore the Malahoodus far, but
left the other birch to thread its cedared soli-
tudes, while we turned back to try our fortunes
in the larger stream. We paddled on about
four miles farther, lingering now and then opposite the black mouth of a moose-path. The
incidents of our voyage were few, but quite as
exciting and profitable as the *items* of the newspapers. A stray log compensated very well
for the ordinary run of accidents, and the floating *carkiss* of a moose which we met could
pass muster instead of a singular discovery of
human remains by workmen in digging a cellar.
Once or twice we saw what seemed ghosts of
trees ; but they turned out to be dead cedars,
in winding-sheets of long gray moss, made
spectral by the moonlight. Just as we were
turning to drift back down-stream, we heard a
loud gnawing sound close by us on the bank.
One of our guides thought it a hedgehog, the

other a bear. I inclined to the bear, as making the adventure more imposing. A rifle was fired at the sound, which began again with the most provoking indifference, ere the echo, flaring madly at first from shore to shore, died far away in a hoarse sigh.

Half past Eleven, P. M. — No sign of a moose yet. The birch, it seems, was strained at the Carry, or the pitch was softened as she lay on the shore during dinner, and she leaks a little. If there be any virtue in the *sitzbad*, I shall discover it. If I cannot extract green cucumbers from the moon's rays, I get something quite as cool. One of the guides shivers so as to shake the birch.

Quarter to Twelve. — *Later from the Freshet!* — The water in the birch is about three inches deep, but the dampness reaches already nearly to the waist. I am obliged to remove the matches from the ground-floor of my trousers into the upper story of a breast-pocket. Meanwhile, we are to sit immovable, — for fear of frightening the moose, — which induces cramps.

Half past Twelve. — A crashing is heard on

the left bank. This is a moose in good earnest. We are besought to hold our breaths, if possible. My fingers so numb, I could not, if I tried. *Crash! crash!* again, and then a plunge, followed by dead stillness. "Swimmin' crik," whispers guide, suppressing all unnecessary parts of speech, — "don't stir." I, for one, am not likely to. A cold fog which has been gathering for the last hour has finished me. I fancy myself one of those naked pigs that seem rushing out of market-doors in winter, frozen in a ghastly attitude of gallop. If I were to be shot myself, I should feel no interest in it. As it is, I am only a spectator, having declined a gun. *Splash!* again; this time the moose is in sight, and *click! click!* one rifle misses fire after the other. The fog has quietly spiked our batteries. The moose goes crashing up the bank, and presently we can hear it chewing its cud close by. So we lie in wait, freezing.

At one o'clock, I propose to land at a deserted *wongen* I had noticed on the way up, where I will make a fire, and leave them to refrigerate as much longer as they please.

Axe in hand, I go plunging through waist-
deep weeds dripping with dew, haunted by
an intense conviction that the gnawing sound
we had heard *was* a bear, and a bear at least
eighteen hands high. There is something pok-
erish about a deserted dwelling, even in broad
daylight ; but here in the obscure wood, and
the moon filtering unwillingly through the
trees ! Well, I made the door at last, and
found the place packed fuller with darkness
than it ever had been with hay. Gradually I
was able to make things out a little, and began to hack frozenly at a log which I groped
out. I was relieved presently by one of the
guides. He cut at once into one of the up-
rights of the building till he got some dry
splinters, and we soon had a fire like the burn-
ing of a whole wood-wharf in our part of the
country. My companion went back to the
birch, and left me to keep house. First I
knocked a hole in the roof (which the fire
began to lick in a relishing way) for a chimney, and then cleared away a damp growth
of " pison-elder," to make a sleeping place.
When the unsuccessful hunters returned, I

had everything quite comfortable, and was
steaming at the rate of about ten horse-power
a minute. Young Telemachus was sorry to
give up the moose so soon, and, with the
teeth chattering almost out of his head, he de-
clared that he would like to stick it out all
night. However, he reconciled himself to the
fire, and, making our beds of some " splits "
which we poked from the roof, we lay down
at half past two. I, who have inherited a
habit of looking into every closet before I go
to bed, for fear of fire, had become in two
days such a stoic of the woods, that I went
to sleep tranquilly, certain that my bedroom
would be in a blaze before morning. And so,
indeed, it was ; and the withes that bound it
together being burned off, one of the sides fell
in without waking me.

Tuesday, 16*th.* — After a sleep of two hours
and a half, so sound that it was as good as
eight, we started at half past four for the hay-
makers' camp again. We found them just
getting breakfast. We sat down upon the
deacon-seat before the fire blazing between the
bedroom and the *salle à manger*, which were

simply two roofs of spruce-bark, sloping to the
ground on one side, the other three being left
open. We found that we had, at least, been
luckier than the other party, for M. had brought
back his convoy without even seeing a moose.
As there was not room at the table for all of
us to breakfast together, these hospitable
woodmen forced us to sit down first, although
we resisted stoutly. Our breakfast consisted
of fresh bread, fried salt pork, stewed whortle-
berries, and tea. Our kind hosts refused to
take money for it, nor would M. accept anything for his trouble. This seemed even more
open-handed when I remembered that they
had brought all their stores over the Carry
upon their shoulders, paying an ache *extra* for
every pound. If their hospitality lacked anything of hard external polish, it had all the
deeper grace which springs only from sincere
manliness. I have rarely sat at a *table d'hôte*
which might not have taken a lesson from
them in essential courtesy. I have never seen
a finer race of men. They have all the virtues
of the sailor, without that unsteady roll in the
gait with which the ocean proclaims itself quite

as much in the moral as in the physical habit of a man. They appeared to me to have hewn out a short northwest passage through wintry woods to those spice-lands of character which we dwellers in cities must reach, if at all, by weary voyages in the monotonous track of the trades.

By the way, as we were embirching last evening for our moose-chase, I asked what I was to do with my baggage. " Leave it here," said our guide, and he laid the bags upon a platform of alders, which he bent down to keep them beyond reach of the rising water.

" Will they be safe here ? "

" As safe as they would be locked up in your house at home."

And so I found them at my return; only the hay-makers had carried them to their camp for greater security against the chances of the weather.

We got back to Kineo in time for dinner; and in the afternoon, the weather being fine, went up the mountain. As we landed at the foot, our guide pointed to the remains of a red shirt and a pair of blanket trousers.

"That," said he, "is the reason there's such a trade in ready-made clo'es. A suit gits pooty well wore out by the time a camp breaks up in the spring, and the lumberers want to look about right when they come back into the settlements, so they buy somethin' ready-made and heave ole bust-up into the bush." True enough, thought I, this is the Ready-made Age. It is quicker being covered than fitted. So we all go to the slop-shop and come out uniformed, every mother's son with habits of thinking and doing cut on one pattern, with no special reference to his peculiar build.

Kineo rises 1750 feet above the sea, and 750 above the lake. The climb is very easy, with fine outlooks at every turn over lake and forest. Near the top is a spring of water, which even Uncle Zeb might have allowed to be wholesome. The little tin dipper was scratched all over with names, showing that vanity, at least, is not put out of breath by the ascent. O Ozymandias, King of kings! We are all scrawling on something of the kind. "My name is engraved on the institutions of my country," thinks the statesman. But,

alas! institutions are as changeable as tin-dip
pers; men are content to drink the same old
water, if the shape of the cup only be new,
and our friend gets two lines in the Biograph-
ical Dictionaries.   After all, these inscrip-
tions, which make us smile up here, are about
as valuable as the Assyrian ones which Hincks
and Rawlinson read at cross-purposes.   Have
we not Smiths and Browns enough, that we
must ransack the ruins of Nimroud for more?
Near the spring we met a Bloomer!   It was
the first chronic one I had ever seen.   It
struck me as a sensible costume for the occa-
sion, and it will be the only wear in the Greek
Kalends, when women believe that sense is an
equivalent for grace.

The forest primeval is best seen from the
top of a mountain.   It then impresses one by
its extent, like an Oriental epic.   To be in it
is nothing, for then an acre is as good as a
thousand square miles.   You cannot see five
rods in any direction, and the ferns, mosses,
and tree-trunks just around you are the best
of it.   As for solitude, night will make a better
one with ten feet square of pitch dark; and

mere size is hardly an element of grandeur,
except in works of man, — as the Colosseum.
It is through one or the other pole of vanity
that men feel the sublime in mountains. It is
either, How small great I am beside it! or,
Big as you are, little I's soul will hold a dozen
of you. The true idea of a forest is not a *selva
selvaggia*, but something humanized a little,
as we imagine the forest of Arden, with trees
standing at royal intervals, — a commonwealth,
and not a communism. To some moods, it is
congenial to look over endless leagues of unbroken savagery without a hint of man.

Wednesday. — This morning fished. Telemachus caught a *laker* of thirteen pounds and
a half, and I an overgrown cusk, which we
threw away, but which I found afterwards
Agassiz would have been glad of, for all is fish
that comes to his net, from the fossil down.
The fish, when caught, are straightway knocked
on the head. A lad who went with us seeming to show an over-zeal in this operation, we
remonstrated. But he gave a good, human
reason for it, — " He no need to ha' gone and
been a fish if he did n't like it," — an excuse

which superior strength or cunning has always found sufficient. It was some comfort, in this case, to think that St. Jerome believed in a limitation of God's providence, and that it did not extend to inanimate things or creatures devoid of reason.

Thus, my dear Storg, I have finished my Oriental adventures, and somewhat, it must be owned, in the diffuse Oriental manner. There is very little about Moosehead Lake in it, and not even the Latin name for moose, which I might have obtained by sufficient research. If 1 had killed one, I would have given you his name in that dead language. I did not profess to give you an account of the lake ; but a journal, and, moreover, *my* journal, with a little nature, a little human nature, and a great deal of I in it, which last ingredient I take to be the true spirit of this species of writing ; all the rest being so much water for tender throats which cannot take it neat.

AT SEA.

AT SEA.

HE sea was meant to be looked at from the shore, as mountains are from the plain. Lucretius made this discovery long ago, and was blunt enough to blurt it forth, romance and sentiment — in other words, the pretence of feeling what we do not feel — being inventions of a later day. To be sure, Cicero used to twaddle about Greek literature and philosophy, much as people do about ancient art nowadays; but I rather sympathize with those stout old Romans who despised both, and believed that to found an empire was as grand an achievement as to build an epic or to carve a statue. But though there might have been twaddle, (as why not, since there was a Senate?) I rather think Pe-

trarch was the first choragus of that sentimental dance which so long led young folks
away from the realities of life like the piper of
Hamelin, and whose succession ended, let us
hope, with Chateaubriand. But for them,
Byron, whose real strength lay in his sincerity,
would never have talked about the " sea bound-
ing beneath him like a steed that knows his
rider," and all that sort of thing. Even if it
had been true, steam has been as fatal to that
part of the romance of the sea as to hand-loom
weaving. But what say you to a twelve days'
calm such as we dozed through in mid-Atlantic
and in mid-August ? I know nothing so tedious
at once and exasperating as that regular slap
of the wilted sails when the ship rises and falls
with the slow breathing of the sleeping sea,
one greasy, brassy swell following another,
slow, smooth, immitigable as the series of
Wordsworth's "Ecclesiastical Sonnets." Even
at his best, Neptune, in a *tête-à-tête*, has a way
of repeating himself, an obtuseness to the *ne
quid nimis*, that is stupefying. It reminds me
of organ-music and my good friend Sebastian
Bach. A fugue or two will do very well; but

a concert made up of nothing else is altogether too epic for me. There is nothing so desperately monotonous as the sea, and I no longer wonder at the cruelty of pirates. Fancy an existence in which the coming up of a clumsy finback whale, who says *Pooh !* to you solemnly as you lean over the taffrail, is an event as exciting as an election on shore ! The dampness seems to strike into the wits as into the lucifer-matches, so that one may scratch a thought half a dozen times and get nothing at last but a faint sputter, the forlorn hope of fire, which only goes far enough to leave a sense of suffocation behind it. Even smoking becomes an employment instead of a solace. Who less likely to come to their wit's end than W. M. T. and A. H. C. ? Yet I have seen them driven to five meals a day for mental occupation. I sometimes sit and pity Noah ; but even he had this advantage over all succeeding navigators, that, wherever he landed, he was sure to get no ill news from home. He should be canonized as the patron-saint of newspaper correspondents, being the only man who ever had the very last authentic intelligence from everywhere.

The finback whale recorded just above has
much the look of a brown-paper parcel, — the
whitish stripes that run across him answering
for the pack-thread. He has a kind of acci-
dental hole in the top of his head, through
which he *pooh-poohs* the rest of creation, and
which looks as if it had been made by the
chance thrust of a chestnut rail. He was our
first event. Our second was harpooning a
sunfish, which basked dozing on the lap of the
sea, looking so much like the giant turtle of
an alderman's dream, that I am persuaded he
would have made mock-turtle soup rather
than acknowledge his imposture. But he
broke away just as they were hauling him
over the side, and sank placidly through the
clear water, leaving behind him a crimson trail
that wavered a moment and was gone.

The sea, though, has better sights than these.
When we were up with the Azores, we began
to meet flying-fish and Portuguese men-of-
war beautiful as the galley of Cleopatra, tiny
craft that dared these seas before Columbus.
I have seen one of the former rise from the
crest of a wave, and, glancing from another

some two hundred feet beyond, take a fresh
flight of perhaps as long. How Calderon
would have similized this pretty creature had
he ever seen it! How would he have run him
up and down the gamut of simile! If a fish,
then a fish with wings; if a bird, then a bird
with fins; and so on, keeping up the poor
shuttle-cock of a conceit as is his wont.
Indeed, the poor thing is the most killing bait
for a comparison, and I assure you I have
three or four in my inkstand; — but be calm,
they shall stay there. Moore, who looked on
all nature as a kind of *Gradus ad Parnassum*,
a *thesaurus* of similitude, and spent his life in
a game of What is my thought like? with
himself, *did* the flying-fish on his way to Ber-
muda. So I leave him in peace.

The most beautiful thing I have seen at sea,
all the more so that I had never heard of it,
is the trail of a shoal of fish through the phosphorescent water. It is like a flight of silver
rockets, or the streaming of northern lights
through that silent nether heaven. I thought
nothing could go beyond that rustling star-
foam which was churned up by our ship's

bows, or those eddies and disks of dreamy
flame that rose and wandered out of sight
behind us.

'T was fire our ship was plunging through,
Cold fire that o'er the quarter flew ;
And wandering moons of idle flame
Grew full and waned, and went and came,
Dappling with light the huge sea-snake
That slid behind us in the wake.

But there was something even more delicately
rare in the apparition of the fish, as they
turned up in gleaming furrows the latent
moonshine which the ocean seemed to have
hoarded against these vacant interlunar nights.
In the Mediterranean one day, as we were
lying becalmed, I observed the water freckled
with dingy specks, which at last gathered to a
pinkish scum on the surface. The sea had
been so phosphorescent for some nights, that
when the Captain gave me my bath, by dous-
ing me with buckets from the house on deck,
the spray flew off my head and shoulders in
sparks. It occurred to me that this dirty-
looking scum might be the luminous matter,
and I had a pailful dipped up to keep till after

dark. When I went to look at it after nightfall, it seemed at first perfectly dead; but
when I shook it, the whole broke out into
what I can only liken to milky flames, whose
lambent silence was strangely beautiful, and
startled me almost as actual projection might an
alchemist. I could not bear to be the death
of so much beauty; so I poured it all over-
board again.

Another sight worth taking a voyage for is
that of the sails by moonlight. Our course
was "south and by east, half south," so that
we seemed bound for the full moon as she
rolled up over our wavering horizon. Then
I used to go forward to the bowsprit and look
back. Our ship was a clipper, with every rag
set, stunsails, sky-scrapers, and all; nor was
it easy to believe that such a wonder could
be built of canvas as that white many-storied
pile of cloud that stooped over me, or drew
back as we rose and fell with the waves.

These are all the wonders I can recall of
my five weeks at sea, except the sun. Were
you ever alone with the sun? You think it a
very simple question; but I never was, in the

full sense of the word, till I was held up to
him one cloudless day on the broad buckler
of the ocean. I suppose one might have the
same feeling in the desert. I remember getting something like it years ago, when I
climbed alone to the top of a mountain, and
lay face up on the hot gray moss, striving to
get a notion of how an Arab might feel. It
was my American commentary of the Koran,
and not a bad one. In a New England winter, too, when everything is gagged with snow,
as if some gigantic physical geographer were
taking a cast of the earth's face in plaster, the
bare knob of a hill will introduce you to the
sun as a comparative stranger. But at sea
you may be alone with him day after day, and
almost all day long. I never understood
before that nothing short of full daylight can
give the supremest sense of solitude. Darkness will not do so, for the imagination peoples it with more shapes than ever were
poured from the frozen loins of the populous
North. The sun, I sometimes think, is a
little *grouty* at sea, especially at high noon,
feeling that he wastes his beams on those

fruitless furrows. It is otherwise with the moon. She "comforts the night," as Chapman finely says, and I always found her a companionable creature.

In the ocean-horizon I took untiring delight. It is the true magic-circle of expectation and conjecture, — almost as good as a wishing-ring. What will rise over that edge we sail toward daily and never overtake? A sail? an island? the new shore of the Old World? Something rose every day, which I need not have gone so far to see, but at whose levee I was a much more faithful courtier than on shore. A cloudless sunrise in mid-ocean is beyond comparison for simple grandeur. It is like Dante's style, bare and perfect. Naked sun meets naked sea, the true classic of nature. There may be more sentiment in morning on shore, — the shivering fairy-jewelry of dew, the silver point-lace of sparkling hoar-frost, — but there is also more complexity, more of the romantic. The one savors of the elder Edda, the other of the Minnesingers.

> And I thus floating, lonely elf,
> A kind of planet by myself,

The mists draw up and furl away,
And in the east a warming gray,
Faint as the tint of oaken woods
When o'er their buds May breathes and broods,
Tells that the golden sunrise-tide
Is lapsing up earth's thirsty side,
Each moment purpling on the crest
Of some stark billow farther west :
And as the sea-moss droops and hears
The gurgling flood that nears and nears,
And then with tremulous content
Floats out each thankful filament,
So waited I until it came,
God's daily miracle, — O shame
That I had seen so many days
Unthankful, without wondering praise,
Not recking more this bliss of earth
Than the cheap fire that lights my hearth !
But now glad thoughts and holy pour
Into my heart, as once a year
To San Miniato's open door,
In long procession, chanting clear,
Through slopes of sun, through shadows hoar,
The coupled monks slow-climbing sing,
And like a golden censer swing
From rear to front, from front to rear
Their alternating bursts of praise,

Till the roof's fading seraphs gaze
Down through an odorous mist, that crawls
Lingeringly up the darkened walls,
And the dim arches, silent long,
Are startled with triumphant song.

I wrote yesterday that the sea still rimmed
our prosy lives with mystery and conjecture.
But one is shut up on shipboard like Mon-
taigne in his tower, with nothing to do but to
review his own thoughts and contradict himself. *Dire, redire, et me contredire,* will be the
staple of my journal till I see land. I say nothing of such matters as the *montagna bruna* on
which Ulysses was wrecked; but since the six-
teenth century could any man reasonably hope
to stumble on one of those wonders which were
cheap as dirt in the days of St. Saga? Faustus,
Don Juan, and Tanhaüser are the last ghosts
of legend, that lingered almost till the Gallic
cock-crow of universal enlightenment and dis-
illusion. The Public School has done for Imagination. What shall I see in Outre-Mer, or
on the way thither, but what can be seen with
eyes? To be sure, I stick by the sea-serpent,

and would fain believe that science has scotched, not killed, him. Nor is he to be lightly given up, for, like the old Scandinavian snake, he binds together for us the two hemispheres of Past and Present, of Belief and Science. He is the link which knits us seaboard Yankees with our Norse progenitors, interpreting between the age of the dragon and that of the railroad train. We have made ducks and drakes of that large estate of wonder and delight bequeathed to us by ancestral vikings, and this alone remains to us unthrift heirs of Linn.

I feel an undefined respect for a man who has seen the sea-serpent. He is to his brother-fishers what the poet is to his fellow-men. Where they have seen nothing better than a school of horse-mackerel, or the idle coils of ocean around Half-way Rock, he has caught authentic glimpses of the withdrawing mantle-hem of the Edda age. I care not for the monster himself. It is not the thing, but the belief in the thing, that is dear to me. May it be long before Professor Owen is comforted with the sight of his unfleshed vertebræ, long before they stretch many a rood behind Kimball's or Barnum's glass, reflected in the shallow orbs of Mr. and Mrs. Public, which stare, but see not! When we read that Captain Spalding, of the pink-stern *Three Pollies*, has beheld him rushing through the brine like an infinite series of bewitched mackerel-casks, we feel that the mystery of old Ocean, at least, has not yet been sounded, — that Faith and Awe survive there unevaporate. I once ventured the horse-mackerel theory to an old fisherman, browner than a tomcod. "Hosmackril!" he exclaimed indignantly, "hosmackril be—" (here he used a phrase commonly indicated in laical literature by the same sign which serves for Doctorate in Divinity,) "don't yer spose *I* know a hos-mackril?" The intonation of that "*I*" would have silenced Professor Monkbarns Owen with his provoking *phoca* forever. What if one should ask *him* if he knew a trilobite?

The fault of modern travellers is, that they see nothing out of sight. They talk of eocene periods and tertiary formations, and tell us how the world looked to the plesiosaur. They

take science (or nescience) with them, instead
of that soul of generous trust their elders had.
All their senses are sceptics and doubters,
materialists reporting things for other sceptics
to doubt still further upon. Nature becomes
a reluctant witness upon the stand, badgered
with geologist hammers and phials of acid.
There have been no travellers since those
included in Hakluyt and Purchas, except
Martin, perhaps, who saw an inch or two into
the invisible at the Orkneys. We have peripatetic lecturers, but no more travellers.
Travellers' stories are no longer proverbial.
We have picked nearly every apple (wormy or
otherwise) from the world's tree of knowledge,
and that without an Eve to tempt us. Two
or three have hitherto hung luckily beyond
reach on a lofty bough shadowing the interior
of Africa, but there is a German Doctor at this
very moment pelting at them with sticks and
stones. It may be only next week, and these
too, bitten by geographers and geologists, will
be thrown away.

Analysis is carried into everything. Even
Deity is subjected to chemic tests. We must

have exact knowledge, a cabinet stuck full of
facts pressed, dried, or preserved in spirits instead of the large, vague world our fathers had.
With them science was poetry; with us, poetry
is science. Our modern Eden is a *hortus sic-
cus*. Tourists defraud rather than enrich us.
They have not that sense of æsthetic propor-
tion which characterized the elder traveller.
Earth is no longer the fine work of art it was,
for nothing is left to the imagination. Job
Hortop, arrived at the height of the Bermudas,
thinks it full time to indulge us in a merman.
Nay, there is a story told by Webster, in his
" Witchcraft," of a merman with a mitre, who,
on being sent back to his watery diocese of fin-
land, made what advances he could toward an
episcopal benediction by bowing his head thrice.
Doubtless he had been consecrated by St.
Antony of Padua. A dumb bishop would be
sometimes no unpleasant phenomenon, by the
way. Sir John Hawkins is not satisfied with
telling us about the merely sensual Canaries,
but is generous enough to throw us in a hand-
ful of " certain flitting islands " to boot.
Henry Hawkes describes the visible Mexican

cities, and then is not so frugal but that he can give us a few invisible ones. Thus do these generous ancient mariners make children of us again. Their successors show us an earth effete and past bearing, tracing out with the eyes of industrious fleas every wrinkle and crowfoot.

The journals of the elder navigators are prose Odysseys. The geographies of our ancestors were works of fancy and imagination. They read poems where we yawn over items. Their world was a huge wonder-horn, exhaustless as that which Thor strove to drain. Ours would scarce quench the small thirst of a bee. No modern voyager brings back the magical foundation-stones of a Tempest. No Marco Polo, traversing the desert beyond the city of Lok, would tell of things able to inspire the mind of Milton with

" Calling shapes and beckoning shadows dire,
And airy tongues that syllable men's names
On sands and shores and desert wildernesses."

It was easy enough to believe the story of Dante, when two thirds of even the upper-

world were yet untraversed and unmapped.
With every step of the recent traveller our
inheritance of the wonderful is diminished.
Those beautifully pictured notes of the Possible are redeemed at a ruinous discount in the
hard and cumbrous coin of the actual. How
are we not defrauded and impoverished? Does
California vie with El Dorado? or are Bruce's
Abyssinian kings a set-off for Prester John?
A bird in the bush is worth two in the hand.
And if the philosophers have not even yet
been able to agree whether the world has any
existence independent of ourselves, how do we
not gain a loss in every addition to the cata-
logue of Vulgar Errors? Where are the
fishes which nidificated in trees? Where the
monopodes sheltering themselves from the sun
beneath their single umbrella-like foot, — umbrella-like in everything but the fatal necessity
of being borrowed? Where the Acephali,
with whom Herodotus, in a kind of ecstasy,
wound up his climax of men with abnormal
top-pieces? Where the Roc whose eggs are
possibly boulders, needing no far-fetched theory of glacier or iceberg to account for them?

Where the tails of the men of Kent ?   Where
the no legs of the bird of paradise ?   Where
the Unicorn, with that single horn of his, sovereign against all manner of poisons ?   Where
the Fountain of Youth ?   Where that Thes-
salian spring, which, without cost to the country, convicted and punished perjurers ?   Where
the Amazons of Orellana ?   All these, and a
thousand other varieties, we have lost, and
have got nothing instead of them.   And those
who have robbed us of them have stolen that
which not enriches themselves.   It is so much
wealth cast into the sea beyond all approach
of diving-bells.   We owe no thanks to Mr. J.
E. Worcester, whose Geography we studied
enforcedly at school.   Yet even he had his
relentings, and in some softer moment vouch-
safed us a fine, inspiring print of the Mael-
strom, answerable to the twenty-four mile
diameter of its suction.   Year by year, more
and more of the world gets disenchanted.
Even the icy privacy of the arctic and antarctic
circles is invaded.   Our youth are no longer
ingenious, as indeed no ingenuity is demanded
of them.   Everything is accounted for, every-

thing cut and dried, and the world may be put together as easily as the fragments of a dissected map. The Mysterious bounds nothing now on the North, South, East, or West. We have played Jack Horner with our earth, till there is never a plum left in it.

THE FARMER'S BOY.

SPRING.

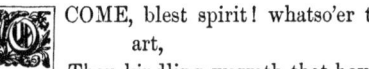COME, blest spirit! whatso'er thou
        art,
    Thou kindling warmth that hover'st
        round my heart,
Sweet inmate, hail ! thou source of sterling
    joy,
That poverty itself cannot destroy,
Be thou my Muse ; and, faithful still to me,
Retrace the paths of wild obscurity.
No deeds of arms my humble lines rehearse ;
No Alpine wonders thunder through my verse,
The roaring cataract, the snow-topt hill,

Inspiring awe, till breath itself stands still :
Nature's sublimer scenes ne'er charmed mine
        eyes,
Nor science led me through the boundless
        skies ;
From meaner objects far my raptures flow ;
O point these raptures ! bid my bosom glow !
And lead my soul to ecstasies of praise
For all the blessings of my infant days !
Bear me through regions where gay Fancy
        dwells ;
But mould to Truth's fair form what Memory
        tells.

Live, trifling incidents, and grace my song,
That to the humblest menial belong :
To him whose drudgery unheeded goes,
His joys unreckoned as his cares or woes ;
Though joys and cares in every path are sown,
And youthful minds have feelings of their
        own,
Quick-springing sorrows, transient as the dew,
Delights from trifles, trifles ever new.
'T was thus with Giles : meek, fatherless,
        and poor :

Labor his portion, but he felt no more;
No stripes, no tyranny his steps pursued :
His life was constant, cheerful servitude :
Strange to the world, he wore a bashful look,
The fields his study, Nature was his book ;
And, as revolving seasons changed the scene
From heat to cold, tempestuous to serene,
Though every change still varied his employ,
Yet each new duty brought its share of joy.

Where noble Grafton spreads his rich do-
  mains,
Round Euston's watered vale and sloping
  plains,
Where woods and groves in solemn grandeur
  rise,
Where the kite brooding unmolested flies,
The woodcock and the painted pheasant race,
And skulking foxes, destined for the chase,
There Giles, untaught and unrepining, strayed
Through every copse, and grove, and winding
  glade ;
There his first thoughts to Nature's charms
  inclined,
That stamps devotion on the inquiring mind.

A little farm his generous master tilled,
Who with peculiar grace his station filled ;
By deeds of hospitality endeared,
Served from affection, for his worth revered ;
A happy offspring blest his plenteous board,
His fields were fruitful, and his barns well
     stored,
And fourscore ewes he fed ; a sturdy team ;
And lowing kine that grazed beside the
     stream :
Unceasing industry he kept in view ;
And never lacked a job for Giles to do.

Fled now the sullen murmurs of the North,
The splendid raiment of the Spring peeps
     forth ;
Her universal green, and the clear sky,
Delight still more and more the gazing eye.
Wide o'er the fields, in rising moisture strong,
Shoots up the simple flower, or creeps along
The mellowed soil ; imbibing fairer hues,
Or sweets from frequent showers and evening
     dews,
That summon from their sheds the slumber-
     ing ploughs,

While health impregnates every breeze that
    blows :
No wheels support the diving, pointed share ;
No groaning ox is doomed to labor there ;
No helpmates teach the docile steed his road
(Alike unknown the ploughboy and the
    goad) ;
But, unassisted through each toilsome day,
With smiling brow the ploughman cleaves
    his way,
Draws his fresh parallels, and, widening still,
Treads slow the heavy dale, or climbs the hill :
Strong on the wind his busy followers play,
Where writhing earthworms meet the unwel-
    come day ;
Till all is changed, and hill and level down
Assume a livery of sober brown ;
Again disturbed, when Giles with wearying
    strides
From ridge to ridge the ponderous harrow
    guides,
His heels deep sinking every step he goes,
Till dirt adhesive loads his clouted shoes.
Welcome, green headland ! firm beneath his
    feet ;

Welcome, the friendly bank's refreshing seat ;
There, warm with toil, his panting horses
    browse
Their sheltering canopy of pendent boughs ;
Till rest, delicious, chase each transient pain,
And new-born vigor swell in every vein.
Hour after hour, and day to day succeeds,
Till every clod and deep-drawn furrow spreads
To crumbling mould, a level surface clear,
And strewed with corn to crown the rising
    year ;
And o'er the whole Giles, once transverse
    again,
In earth's moist bosom buries up the grain.
The work is done : no more to man is given ;
The grateful farmer trusts the rest to Heaven.
Yet oft with anxious heart he looks around,
And marks the first green blade that breaks
    the ground ;
In fancy sees his trembling oats uprun,
His tufted barley yellow with the sun ;
Sees clouds propitious shed their timely store,
And all his harvest gathered round his door.
But still unsafe the big swoln grain below,
A favorite morsel with the rook and crow ;

From field to field the flock increasing goes;
To level crops most formidable foes :
Their danger well the wary plunderers know,
And place a watch on some conspicuous
        bough ;
Yet oft the skulking gunner by surprise
Will scatter death amongst them as they rise.
These, hung in triumph round the spacious
        field,
At best will but a short-lived terror yield :
Nor guards of property (not penal law,
But harmless riflemen of rags and straw) ;
Familiarized to these they boldly rove,
Nor heed such sentinels that never move.
Let then your birds lie prostrate on the earth,
In dying posture, and with wings stretcht
        forth !
Shift them at eve or morn from place to place,
And death shall terrify the pilfering race ;
In the mid air, while circling round and
        round,
They call their lifeless comrades from the
        ground ;
With quickening wing, and notes of loud
        alarm,

Warn the whole flock to shun the impending
    harm.
  This task had Giles, in fields remote from
    home ;
Oft has he wished the rosy morn to come :
Yet never famed was he nor foremost found
To break the seal of sleep ; his sleep was
    sound :
But when at daybreak summoned from his
    bed,
Light as the lark that carolled o'er his
    head.
His sandy way, deep-worn by hasty showers,
O'erarched with oaks that formed fantastic
    bowers,
Waving aloft their towering branches proud,
In borrowed tinges from the eastern cloud,
Gave inspiration, pure as ever flowed,
And genuine transport in his bosom glowed.
His own shrill matin joined the various notes
Of Nature's music, from a thousand throats :
The blackbird strove with emulation sweet,
And Echo answered from her close retreat ,
The sporting white-throat, on some twig's end
    borne,

Poured hymns to freedom and the rising
    morn ;
Stopt in her song, perchance the starting
    thrush
Shook a white shower from the blackthorn-
    bush,
Where dew-drops thick as early blossoms
    hung,
And trembled as the minstrel sweetly sung.
Across his path, in either grove to hide,
The timid rabbit scouted by his side ;
Or pheasant boldly stalked along the road,
Whose gold and purple tints alternate glowed.

But groves no farther fenced the devious
    way ;
A wide-extended heath before him lay,
Where on the grass the stagnant shower had
    run,
And shone a mirror to the rising sun,
Thus doubly seen to light a distant wood,
To give new life to each expanding bud ;
And chase away the dewy foot-marks found,
Where prowling Reynard trod his nightly
    round ;

To shun whose thefts 't was Giles's evening
    care,
His feathered victims to suspend in air,
High on the bough that nodded o'er his
    head,
And thus each morn to strew the field with
    dead.

  His simple errand done, he homeward
    hies ;
Another instantly its place supplies.
The clattering dairy-maid immersed in steam,
Singing and scrubbing, midst her milk and
    cream,
Bawls out, " Go fetch the cows ! " — he hears
    no more ;
For pigs, and ducks, and turkeys throng the
    door,
And sitting hens, for constant war prepared ;
A concert strange to that which late he heard.
Straight to the meadow then he whistling
    goes ;
With well-known halloo calls his lazy cows :
Down the rich pasture heedlessly they graze,
Or hear the summons with an idle gaze ;

For well they know the cow-yard yields no
    more
Its tempting fragrance, nor its wintry store.
Reluctance marks their steps, sedate and
    slow !
The right of conquest all the law they know ;
The strong press on, the weak by turns suc-
    ceed,
And one superior always takes the lead ;
Is ever foremost, wheresoe'er they stray ;
Allowed precedence, undisputed sway ;
With jealous pride her station is maintained,
For many a broil that post of honor gained.
At home, the yard affords a grateful scene ;
For Spring makes e'en a miry cow-yard clean.
Thence from its chalky bed behold con-
    veyed
The rich manure that drenching Winter made,
Which, piled near home, grows green with
    many a weed,
A promised nutriment for Autumn's seed.
Forth comes the maid, and like the morning
    smiles ;
The mistress too, and followed close by Giles.
A friendly tripod forms their humble seat,

With pails bright scoured, and delicately
    sweet.
Where shadowing elms obstruct the morning
    ray,
Begins the work, begins the simple lay ;
The full-charged udder yields its willing
    streams,
While Mary sings some lover's amorous
    dreams ;
And crouching Giles beneath a neighboring
    tree
Tugs o'er his pail, and chants with equal
    glee ;
Whose hat with tattered brim, of nap so bare,
From the cow's side purloins a coat of hair,
A mottled ensign of his harmless trade,
An unambitious, peaceable cockade.
As unambitious too that cheerful aid
The mistress yields beside her rosy maid ;
With joy she views her plenteous reeking
    store,
And bears a brimmer to the dairy door :
Her cows dismissed, the luscious mead to
    roam,
Till eve again recall them loaded home.

And now the dairy claims her choicest care,
And half her household find employment
    there :
Slow rolls the churn, its load of clogging
    cream
At once foregoes its quality and name :
From knotty particles first floating wide,
Congealing butter's dashed from side to side ;
Streams of new milk through flowing coolers
    stray,
And snow-white curd abounds, and whole-
    some whey.
Due north the unglazed windows, cold and
    clear,
For warming sunbeams are unwelcome here.
Brisk goes the work beneath each busy hand,
And Giles must trudge, whoever gives com-
    mand ;
A Gibeonite that serves them all by turns :
He drains the pump, from him the fagot
    burns ;
From him the noisy hogs demand their food ;
While at his heels run many a chirping brood,
Or down his path in expectation stand,
With equal claims upon his strewing hand.

Thus wastes the morn, till each with pleasure
 sees
The bustle o'er, and pressed the new-made
 cheese.

 Unrivalled stands thy country cheese, O
  Giles!
Whose very name alone engenders smiles ;
Whose fame abroad by every tongue is
 spoke,
The well-known butt of many a flinty joke,
That pass like current coin the nation
  through ;
And, ah! experience proves the satire true.
Provision's grave, thou ever-craving mart,
Dependent, huge metropolis! where Art
Her poring thousands stows in breathless
  rooms,
Midst poisonous smokes, and steams, and
  rattling looms :
Where Grandeur revels in unbounded stores ;
Restraint, a slighted stranger at their doors !
Thou, like a whirlpool, drain'st the countries
  round,
Till London market, London price, resound

Through every town, round every passing
    load,
And dairy produce throngs the eastern road :
Delicious veal and butter, every hour,
From Essex lowlands, and the banks of Stour ;
And further far, where numerous herds re-
    pose,
From Orwell's brink, from Waveny, or Ouse.
Hence Suffolk dairy-wives run mad for cream,
And leave their milk with nothing but its
    name ;
Its name derision and reproach pursue,
And strangers tell of "three times skimmed
    sky-blue."
To cheese converted, what can be its boast ?
What, but the common virtues of a post !
If drought o'ertake it faster than the knife,
Most fair it bids for stubborn length of life,
And, like the oaken shelf whereon 't is laid,
Mocks the weak efforts of the bending blade ;
Or in the hog-trough rests in perfect spite,
Too big to swallow, and too hard to bite.
Inglorious victory ! Ye Cheshire meads,
Or Severn's flowery dales, where plenty
    treads,

Was your rich milk to suffer wrongs like
        these,
Farewell your pride! farewell, renownéd
        cheese!
The skimmer dread, whose ravages alone
Thus turn the meads' sweet nectar into stone.

Neglected now the early daisy lies;
Nor thou, pale primrose, bloom'st the only
        prize:
Advancing Spring profusely spreads abroad
Flowers of all hues, with sweetest fragrance
        stored;
Where'er she treads Love gladdens every plain,
Delight on tiptoe bears her lucid train;
Sweet Hope with conscious brow before her
        flies,
Anticipating wealth from Summer skies;
All nature feels her renovating sway;
The sheep-fed pasture, and the meadow gay;
And trees and shrubs, no longer budding seen,
Display the new-grown branch of lighter
        green;
On airy downs the idling shepherd lies,
And sees to-morrow in the marbled skies.

Here then, my soul, thy darling theme pursue,
For every day was Giles a shepherd too.

Small was his charge : no wilds had they
    to roam ;
But bright enclosures circling round their
    home.
No yellow-blossomed furze nor stubborn
    thorn,
The heath's rough produce, had their fleeces
    torn ;
Yet ever roving, ever seeking thee,
Enchanting spirit, dear Variety !
O happy tenants, prisoners of a day !
Released to ease, to pleasure, and to play ;
Indulged through every field by turns to
    range,
And taste them all in one continual change.
For though luxuriant their grassy food,
Sheep long confined but loathe the present
    good :
Bleating around the homeward gate they meet,
And starve, and pine, with plenty at their
    feet.
Loosed from the winding lane, a joyful throng,

See, o'er yon pasture, how they pour along !
Giles round their boundaries takes his usual
  stroll ;
Sees every pass secured, and fences whole ;
High fences, proud to charm the gazing eye,
Where many a nestling first essays to fly ;
Where blows the woodbine, faintly streaked
  with red,
And rests on every bough its tender head ;
Round the young ash its twining branches
  meet,
Or crown the hawthorn with its odor sweet.

 Say, ye that know, ye who have felt and
  seen,
Spring's morning smiles, and soul-enlivening
  green,
Say, did you give the thrilling transport way ?
Did your eye brighten when young lambs at
  play
Leaped o'er your path with animated pride,
Or gazed in merry clusters by your side ?
Ye who can smile, to wisdom no disgrace,
At the arch meaning of a kitten's face :
If spotless innocence, and infant mirth,

Excites to praise, or gives reflection birth ;
In shades like these pursue your favorite joy,
Midst Nature's revels, sports that never cloy.

A few begin a short but vigorous race,
And Indolence, abashed, soon flies the place ;
Thus challenged forth, see thither one by one,
From every side assembling playmates run ;
A thousand wily antics mark their stay,
A starting crowd, impatient of delay.
Like the fond dove from fearful prison freed,
Each seems to say, " Come, let us try our
          speed " ;
Away they scour, impetuous, ardent, strong,
The green turf trembling as they bound
          along ;
Adown the slope, then up the hillock climb,
Where every molehill is a bed of thyme ;
There panting stop ; yet scarcely can refrain ;
A bird, a leaf will set them off again ;
Or, if a gale with strength unusual blow,
Scattering the wild-brier roses into snow,
Their little limbs increasing efforts try,
Like the torn flower the fair assemblage fly.
Ah, fallen rose ! sad emblem of their doom ;

Frail as thyself, they perish as they bloom !
Though unoffending Innocence may plead,
Though frantic ewes may mourn the savage
    deed,
Their shepherd comes, a messenger of blood,
And drives them bleating from their sports
    and food.
Care loads his brow, and pity wrings his heart
For lo, the murdering butcher, with his cart.
Demands the firstlings of his flock to die,
And makes a sport of life and liberty !
His gay companions Giles beholds no more ;
Closed are their eyes, their fleeces drenched
    in gore ;
Nor can compassion, with her softest notes,
Withhold the knife that plunges through
    their throats.

    Down, indignation ! hence, ideas foul !
Away the shocking image from my soul !
Let kindlier visitants attend my way,
Beneath the approaching Summer's fervid ray;
Nor thankless glooms obtrude, nor cares an-
    noy,
Whilst the sweet theme is universal joy.

SUMMER.

THE farmer's life displays in every
   part
  A moral lesson to the sensual heart,
Though in the lap of Plenty, thoughtful still,
He looks beyond the present good or ill ;
Nor estimates alone one blessing's worth
From changeful seasons, or capricious earth,
But views the future with the present hours,
And looks for failures as he looks for showers ;
For casual as for certain want prepares,
And round his yard the reeking haystack
   rears ;

Or clover, blossomed lovely to the sight,
His team's rich store through many a wintry
 night.
What though abundance round his dwelling
 spreads,
Though, ever moist, his self-improving meads
Supply his dairy with a copious flood,
And seem to promise unexhausted food ;
That promise fails, when buried deep in
 snow,
And vegetative juices cease to flow.
And this his plough turns up with destined
 lands,
Whence stormy Winter draws its full de-
 mands ;
For this, the seed minutely small he sows,
Whence, sound and sweet, the hardy turnip
 grows.
But how unlike to April's closing days !
High climbs the sun, and darts his powerful
 rays :
Whitens the fresh-drawn mould, and pierces
 through
The cumbrous clods that tumble round the
 plough.

O'er heaven's bright azure hence with joyful
    eyes
The farmer sees dark clouds assembling rise :
Borne o'er his fields a heavy torrent falls,
And strikes the earth in hasty driving squalls.
" Right welcome down, ye precious drops," he
    cries ;
But soon, too soon, the partial blessing flies.
" Boy, bring the harrows, try how deep the
    rain
Has forced its way." He comes, but comes
    in vain ;
Dry dust beneath the bubbling surface lurks,
And mocks the pains the more, the more he
    works :
Still, midst huge clods, he plunges on forlorn,
That laugh his harrows and the shower to
    scorn.
E'en thus the living clod, the stubborn fool,
Resists the stormy lectures of the school,
Till tried with gentler means, the dunce to
    please,
His head imbibes right reason by degrees ;
As when from eve till morning's wakeful
    hour,

Light constant rain evinces secret power,
And ere the day resumes its wonted smiles,
Presents a cheerful, easy task for Giles.
Down with a touch the mellowed soil is laid,
And yon tall crop next claims his timely
      aid ;
Thither well pleased he hies, assured to find
Wild, trackless haunts, and objects to his
      mind.

  Shot up from broad rank blades that droop
      below,
The nodding wheat-ear forms a graceful bow,
With milky kernels starting full, weighed
      down,
Ere yet the sun hath tinged its head with
      brown ;
There thousands in a flock, forever gay,
Loud chirping sparrows welcome on the day,
And from the mazes of the leafy thorn
Drop one by one upon the bending corn.
Giles with a pole assails their close retreats,
And round the grass-grown dewy border
      beats ;
On either side completely overspread,

Here branches bend, their corn o'ertops his
    head.
Green covert, hail ! for through the varying
    year
No hours so sweet, no scene to him so dear.
Here Wisdom's placid eye delighted sees
His frequent intervals of lonely ease,
And with one ray his infant soul inspires,
Just kindling there her never-dying fires,
Whence solitude derives peculiar charms,
And heaven-directed thought his bosom
    warms.
Just where the parting bough's light shad-
    ows play,
Scarce in the shade, nor in the scorching day,
Stretched on the turf he lies, a peopled bed,
Where swarming insects creep around his
    head.
The small dust-colored beetle climbs with
    pain,
O'er the smooth plantain-leaf, a spacious
    plain !
Thence higher still, by countless steps con-
    veyel,
He gains the summit of a shivering blade,

And flirts his filmy wings, and looks around,
Exulting in his distance from the ground.
The tender speckled moth here dancing seen,
The vaunting grasshopper of glossy green.
And all prolific Summer's sporting train,
Their little lives by various powers sustain.
But what can unassisted vision do ?
What but recoil where most it would pursue ;
His patient gaze but finish with a sigh,
When Music waking speaks the skylark nigh !
Just starting from the corn, he cheerly sings,
And trusts with conscious pride his downy
            wings ;
Still louder breathes, and in the face of day
Mounts up, and calls on Giles to mark his
            way.
Close to his eyes his hat he instant bends,
And forms a friendly telescope that lends
Just aid enough to dull the glaring light,
And place the wandering bird before his sight,
That oft beneath a light cloud sweeps along,
Lost for a while, yet pours the varied song :
The eye still follows, and the cloud moves by,
Again he stretches up the clear blue sky ;
His form, his motion, undistinguished quite,

Save when he wheels direct from shade to
    light :
E'en then the songster a mere speck became,
Gliding like fancy's bubbles in a dream,
The gazer sees ; but, yielding to repose,
Unwittingly his jaded eyelids close.
Delicious sleep ! from sleep who could for-
    bear,
With no more guilt than Giles, and no more
    care ?
Peace o'er his slumbers waves her guardian
    wing,
Nor conscience once disturbs him with a
    sting ;
He wakes refreshed from every trivial pain,
And takes his pole, and brushes round again.

Its dark-green hue, its sicklier tints, all fail
And ripening harvest rustles in the gale.
A glorious sight, if glory dwells below,
Where Heaven's munificence makes all the
    show
O'er every field and golden prospect found,
That glads the ploughman's Sunday morn-
    ing's round,

When on some eminence he takes his stand.
To judge the smiling produce of the land.

Here Vanity slinks back, her head to hide :
What is there here to flatter human pride ?
The towering fabric, or the dome's loud roar,
And steadfast columns, may astonish more,
Where the charmed gazer long delighted stays,
Yet traced but to the architect the praise ;
Whilst here, the veriest clown that treads the
        sod,
Without one scruple gives the praise to God ;
And twofold joys possess his raptured mind,
From gratitude and admiration joined.

  Here, midst the boldest triumphs of her
        worth,
Nature herself invites the reapers forth ;
Dares the keen sickle from its twelvemonth's
        rest,
And gives that ardor which in every breast,
From infancy to age, alike appears,
When the first sheaf its plumy top uprears.
No rake takes here what Heaven to all be-
        stows —
Children of want, for you the bounty flows !

And every cottage from the plenteous store
Receives a burden nightly at his door.

   Hark! where the sweeping scythe now
      rips along,
Each sturdy mower, emulous and strong,
Whose writhing form meridian heat defies,
Bends o'er his work, and every sinew tries;
Prostrates the waving treasure at his feet,
But spares the rising clover, short and sweet.
Come, Health! come, Jollity! light-footed,
     come;
Here hold your revels, and make this your
     home.
Each heart awaits and hails you as its own;
Each moistened brow that scorns to wear a
     frown;
The unpeopled dwelling mourns its tenant
     strayed;
E'en the domestic laughing dairy-maid
Hies to the field, the general toil to share.
Meanwhile the farmer quits his elbow-chair,
His cool brick floor, his pitcher, and his ease,
And braves the sultry beams, and gladly sees
His gates thrown open, and his team abroad,

The ready group attendant on his word,
To turn the swath, the quivering load to rear,
Or ply the busy rake, the land to clear.
Summer's light garb itself now cumbrous
    grown,
Each his thin doublet in the shade throws
    down ;
Where oft the mastiff skulks with half-shut
    eye,
And rouses at the stranger passing by ;
Whilst unrestrained the social converse flows,
And every breast Love's powerful impulse
    knows,
And rival wits with more than rustic grace
Confess the presence of a pretty face.

For, lo ! encircled there, the lovely maid,
In youth's own bloom and native smiles ar-
    rayed ;
Her hat awry, divested of her gown,
Her creaking stays of leather, stout and
    brown ; —
Invidious barrier ! Why art thou so high,
When the slight covering of her neck slips by,
There half revealing to the eager sight

Her full, ripe bosom, exquisitely white?
In many a local tale of harmless mirth,
And many a jest of momentary birth,
She bears a part, and as she stops to speak,
Strokes back the ringlets from her glowing
        cheek.

Now noon gone by, and four declining
        hours,
The weary limbs relax their boasted powers;
Thirst rages strong, the fainting spirits fail,
And ask the sovereign cordial, home-brewed
        ale :
Beneath some sheltering heap of yellow corn
Rests the hooped keg, and friendly cooling
        horn,
That mocks alike the goblet's brittle frame,
Its costlier portions, and its nobler name.
To Mary first the brimming draught is given,
By toil made welcome as the dews of heaven,
And never lip that pressed its homely edge
Had kinder blessings or a heartier pledge.

Of wholesome viand here a banquet smiles,
A common cheer for all ; — e'en humble
        Giles,

Who joys his trivial services to yield
Amidst the fragrance of the open field ;
Oft doomed in suffocating heat to bear
The cobwebbed barn's impure and dusty air ;
To ride in murky state the panting steed,
Destined aloft the unloaded grain to tread,
Where, in his path, as heaps on heaps are
   thrown,
He rears and plunges the loose mountain
   down :
Laborious task ! with what delight, when
   done,
Both horse and rider greet the unclouded sun !

Yet by the unclouded sun are hourly bred
The bold assailants that surround thine head,
Poor, patient Ball ! and with insulting wing
Roar in thine ears, and dart the piercing sting ;
In thy behalf the crest-waved boughs avail
More than thy short-clipt remnant of a tail,
A moving mockery, a useless name,
A living proof of cruelty and shame.
Shame to the man, whatever fame he bore,
Who took from thee what man can ne'er re-
   store,

Thy weapon of defence, thy chiefest good,
When swarming flies contending suck thy
    blood.
Nor thine alone the suffering, thine the care,
The fretful ewe bemoans an equal share ;
Tormented into sores, her head she hides,
Or angry sweeps them from her new-shorn
    sides.
Penned in the yard, e'en now at closing day
Unruly cows with marked impatience stay,
And, vainly striving to escape their foes,
The pail kick down ; a piteous current flows.

Is 't not enough that plagues like these
    molest ?
Must still another foe annoy their rest ?
He comes, the pest and terror of the yard,
His full-fledged progeny's imperious guard ;
The gander ; — spiteful, insolent and bold,
At the colt's footlock takes his daring hold ;
There, serpent-like, escapes a dreadful blow ;
And straight attacks a poor defenceless cow :
Each booby goose the unworthy strife enjoys,
And hails his prowess with redoubled noise.
Then back he stalks, of self-importance full,

Seizes the shaggy foretop of the bull,
Till, whirled aloft, he falls : a timely check,
Enough to dislocate his worthless neck :
For lo ! of old he boasts an honored wound ;
Behold that broken wing that trails the
    ground !
Thus fools and bravoes kindred pranks pur-
    sue ;
As savage quite, and oft as fatal too.
Happy the man that foils an envious elf,
Using the darts of spleen to serve himself.
As when by turns the strolling swine engage
The utmost efforts of the bully's rage,
Whose nibbling warfare on the grunter's side
Is welcome pleasure to his bristly hide ;
Gently he stoops, or, stretched at ease along,
Enjoys the insults of the gabbling throng,
That march exulting round his fallen head,
As human victors trample on their dead.

Still Twilight, welcome !   Rest, how sweet
    art thou !
Now eve o'erhangs the western cloud's thick
    brow :
The far-stretched curtain of retiring light,

With fiery treasures fraught ; that on the
　　sight
Flash from its bulging sides, where darkness
　　lowers,
In fancy's eye, a chain of mouldering towers ;
Or craggy coasts just rising into view,
Midst javelins dire, and darts of streaming
　　blue.

　Anon tired laborers bless their sheltering
　　home,
When midnight and the frightful tempest
　　come.
The farmer wakes, and sees, with silent dread,
The angry shafts of Heaven gleam round his
　　bed ;
The bursting cloud reiterated roars,
Shakes his straw roof, and jars his bolting
　　doors :
The slow-winged storm along the troubled
　　skies
Spreads its dark course ; the wind begins to
　　rise ;
And full-leafed elms, his dwelling's shade by
　　day,

With mimic thunder give its fury way :
Sounds in his chimney-top a doleful peal
Midst pouring rain, or gusts of rattling hail :
With tenfold danger low the tempest bends,
And quick and strong the sulphurous flame
        descends :
The frightened mastiff from his kennel flies,
And cringes at the door with piteous cries.

  Where now 's the trifler ? where the child
        of pride ?
These are the moments when the heart is
        tried !
Nor lives the man, with conscience e'er so
        clear,
But feels a solemn, reverential fear ;
Feels too a joy relieve his aching breast,
When the spent storm hath howled itself to
        rest,
Still, welcome beats the long-continued
        shower,
And, sleep protracted, comes with double
        power ;
Calm dreams of bliss bring on the morning sun,
For every barn is filled, and harvest done !

Now, ere sweet summer bids its long adieu,
And winds blow keen where late the blossom
    grew,
The bustling day and jovial night must come,
The long-accustomed feast of harvest-home.
No blood-stained victory, in story bright,
Can give the philosophic mind delight ;
No triumph please, while rage and death de-
    stroy :
Reflection sickens at the monstrous joy.
And where the joy, if rightly understood,
Like cheerful praise for universal good ?
The soul nor check nor doubtful anguish
    knows,
But free and pure the grateful current flows.

Behold the sound oak table's massy frame
Bestride the kitchen floor ! the careful dame
And generous host invite their friends around,
For all that cleared the crop, or tilled the
    ground,
Are guests by right of custom ; — old and
    young ;
And many a neighboring yeoman join the
    throng,

With artisans that lent their dexterous aid,
When o'er each field the flaming sunbeams
        played.

   Yet Plenty reigns, and from her boundless
        hoard,
Though not one jelly trembles on the board,
Supplies the feast with all that sense can
        crave ;
With all that made our great forefathers brave,
Ere the cloyed palate countless flavors tried,
And cooks had Nature's judgment set aside.
With thanks to Heaven, and tales of rustic
        lore,
The mansion echoes when the banquet's o'er ;
A wider circle spreads and smiles abound,
As quick the frothing horn performs its
        round ;
Care's mortal foe ; that sprightly joys imparts
To cheer the frame and elevate their hearts.
Here, fresh and brown, the hazel's produce lies
In tempting heaps, and peals of laughter rise ;
And crackling music, with the frequent song,
Unheeded bear the midnight hour along.
   Here once a year distinction lowers its
        crest :

The master, servant, and the merry guest
Are equal all ; and round the happy ring
The reaper's eyes exulting glances fling,
And, warmed with gratitude, he quits his
    place,
With sunburnt hands and ale-enlivened face,
Refills the jug his honored host to tend,
To serve at once the master and the friend ;
Proud thus to meet his smiles, to share his
    tale,
His nuts, his conversation, and his ale.

    Such were the days, — of days long past I
      sing,
When pride gave place to mirth without a
    sting ;
Ere tyrant customs strength sufficient bore
To violate the feelings of the poor ;
To leave them distanced in the madd'ning race,
Where'er refinement shows its hated face :
Nor causeless hated ; — 't is the peasant's
    curse,
That hourly makes his wretched station
    worse ;
Destroys life's intercourse ; the social plan

That rank to rank cements, as man to man :
Wealth flows around him, Fashion lordly
    reigns :
Yet poverty is his, and mental pains.

    Methinks I hear the mourner thus impart
The stifled murmurs of his wounded heart :
" Whence comes this change, ungracious, irk-
    some, cold ?
Whence the new grandeur that mine eyes
    behold ?
The widening distance which I daily see,
Has Wealth done this ? — then Wealth's a
    foe to me :
Foe to our rights ; that leaves a powerful few
The paths of emulation to pursue : —
For emulation stoops to us no more :
The hope of humble industry is o'er ;
The blameless hope, the cheering sweet pres-
    age
Of future comforts for declining age.
Can my sons share from this paternal hand
The profits with the labors of the land ?
No, though indulgent Heaven its blessing
    deigns,

Where 's the small farm to suit my scanty
    means ?
Content, the poet sings, with us resides ;
In lonely cots like mine, the damsel hides ;
And will he then in raptured visions tell
That sweet content with want can never dwell ?
A barley loaf, 't is true, my table crowns,
That, fast diminishing in lusty rounds,
Stops Nature's cravings ; yet her sighs will flow
From knowing this, — that once it was not so.
Our annual feast, when Earth her plenty
    yields,
When crowned with boughs the last load quits
    the fields,
The aspect still of ancient joy puts on ;
The aspect only, with the substance gone :
The selfsame horn is still at our command,
But serves none now but the plebeian hand ;
For home-brewed ale, neglected and debased,
Is quite discarded from the realms of taste.
Where unaffected freedom charmed the soul,
The separate table, and the costly bowl,
Cool as the blast that checks the budding
    Spring,
A mockery of gladness round them fling.

For oft the farmer, ere his heart approves,
Yields up the custom which he dearly loves ;
Refinement forces on him like a tide ;
Bold innovations down its current ride,
That bear no peace beneath their showy dress,
Nor add one title to his happiness.
His guests selected, rank's punctilios known ;
What trouble waits upon a casual frown !
Restraint's foul manacles his pleasures maim ;
Selected guests selected phrases claim :
Nor reigns that joy, when hand in hand they
          join,
That good old master felt in shaking mine.
Heaven bless his memory ! bless his honored
          name !
(The poor will speak his lasting worthy
          fame :)
To souls fair-purposed strength and guidance
          give ;
In pity to us still let goodness live :
Let labor have its due ! my cot shall be
From chilling want and guilty murmurs free.
Let labor have its due ; then peace is mine,
And never, never shall my heart repine."

AUTUMN.

ACORNS. HOGS IN THE WOOD. WHEAT-SOWING. THE CHURCH. VILLAGE GIRLS. THE MAD GIRL. THE BIRD-BOY'S HUT. DISAPPOINTMENT, REFLECTIONS, ETC. EUSTON-HALL. FOX-HUNTING. OLD TROUNCER. LONG NIGHTS. A WELCOME TO WINTER.

GAIN, the year's decline, midst storms
    and floods,
The thundering chase, the yellow
    fading woods,
Invite my song ; that fain would boldly tell
Of upland coverts and the echoing dell.
By turns resounding loud, at eve and morn,
The swineherd's halloo, or the huntsman's
    horn.

No more the fields with scattered grain
    supply

The restless wandering tenants of the sty ;
From oak to oak they run with eager haste,
And wrangling share the first delicious taste
Of fallen acorns ; yet but thinly found
Till the strong gale has shook them to the
    ground.
It comes ; and roaring woods obedient wave:
Their home well pleased the joint adventur-
    ers leave:
The trudging sow leads forth her numerous
    young,
Playful, and white, and clean, the briers
    among,
Till briers and thorns increasing fence them
    round,
Where last year's smouldering leaves bestrew
    the ground,
And o'er their heads, loud lashed by furious
    squalls,
Bright from their cups the rattling treasure
    falls ;
Hot, thirsty food ; whence doubly sweet and
    cool
The welcome margin of some rush-grown
    pool,

The wild duck's lonely haunt, whose jealous
    eye
Guards every point ; who sits, prepared to fly,
On the calm bosom of her little lake,
Too closely screened for ruffian winds to
    shake ;
And as the bold intruders press around,
At once she starts, and rises with a bound :
With bristles raised, the sudden noise they
    hear,
And ludicrously wild, and winged with fear,
The herd decamp with more than swinish
    speed,
And snorting dash through sedge, and rush,
    and reed :
Through tangling thickets headlong on they
    go,
Then stop and listen for their fancied foe ;
The hindmost still the growing panic spreads,
Repeated fright the first alarm succeeds,
Till Folly's wages, wounds and thorns, they
    reap :
Yet glorying in their fortunate escape,
Their groundless terrors by degrees soon
    cease,

And Night's dark reign restores their wonted
    peace.
For now the gale subsides, and from each
    bough
The roosting pheasant's short but frequent
    crow
Invites to rest ; and, huddling side by side,
The herd in closest ambush seek to hide ;
Seek some warm slope with shagged moss
    o'erspread,
Dried leaves their copious covering and their
    bed :
In vain may Giles, through gathering glooms
    that fall,
And solemn silence, urge his piercing call :
Whole days and nights they tarry midst
    their store,
Nor quit the woods till oaks can yield no more.

  Beyond bleak Winter's rage, beyond the
  . Spring
That rolling Earth's unvarying course will
    bring,
Who tills the ground looks on with mental
    eye,

And sees next Summer's sheaves and cloud-
    less sky ;
And even now, whilst Nature's beauty dies,
Deposits seed, and bids new harvests rise ;
Seed well prepared, and warmed with glow-
    ing lime,
'Gainst earth-bred grubs, and cold, and lapse
    of time :
For searching frosts and various ills invade,
Whilst wintry months depress the springing
    blade.
The plough moves heavily, and strong the
    soil,
And clogging harrows with augmented toil
Dive deep : and clinging, mixes with the
    mould
A fattening treasure from the nightly fold,
And all the cow-yard's highly valued store
That late bestrewed the blackened surface
    o'er.
No idling hours are here, when Fancy trims
Her dancing taper over outstretched limbs,
And, in her thousand thousand colors drest,
Plays round the grassy couch of noontide rest:
Here Giles for hours of indolence atones

With strong exertion and with weary bones,
And knows no leisure ; till the distant chime
Of Sabbath bells he hears at sermon-time,
That down the brook sound sweetly in the
          gale,
Or strike the rising hill, or skim the dale.

  Nor his alone the sweets of ease to taste :
Kind rest extends to all : — save one poor
          beast,
That, true to time and pace, is doomed to
          plod,
To bring the pastor to the house of God :
Mean structure : where no bones of heroes
          lie !
The rude inelegance of poverty
Reigns here alone : else why that roof of
          straw ?
Those narrow windows with the frequent
          flaw ?
O'er whose low cells the dock and mallow
          spread,
And rampant nettles lift the spiry head,
Whilst from the hollows of the tower on high
The gray-capped daws in saucy legions fly.

Round these lone walls assembling neigh-
    bors meet,
And tread departed friends beneath their feet;
And new-briered graves, that prompt the se-
    cret sigh,
Show each the spot where he himself must lie.

Midst timely greetings village news goes
    round,
Of crops late shorn, or crops that deck the
    ground ;
Experienced ploughmen in the circle join ;
While sturdy boys, in feats of strength to
    shine,
With pride elate, their young associates brave
To jump from hollow-sounding grave to
    grave ;
Then close consulting, each his talent lends
To plan fresh sports when tedious service ends.

Hither at times, with cheerfulness of soul,
Sweet village maids from neighboring hamlets
    stroll,
That, like the light-heeled does o'er lawns
    that rove,

Look shyly curious ; ripening into love ;
For love 's their errand : hence the tints that
    glow
On either cheek, a heightened lustre know :
When, conscious of their charms, e'en Age
    looks sly,
And rapture beams from Youth's observant
    eye.

The pride of such a party, Nature's pride,
Was lovely Poll ; who innocently tried,
With hat of airy shape and ribbons gay,
Love to inspire, and stand in Hymen's way :
But, ere her twentieth summer could ex-
    pand,
Or youth was rendered happy with her hand,
Her mind's serenity, her peace was gone,
Her eye grew languid and she wept alone :
Yet causeless seemed her grief ; for quick re-
    strained,
Mirth followed loud ; or indignation reigned :
Whims wild and simple led her from her
    home,
The heath, the common, or the fields to roam:
Terror and joy alternate ruled her hours ;

Now blithe she sung, and gathered useless
    flowers ;
Now plucked a tender twig from every bough,
To whip the hovering demons from her brow.
Ill-fated maid ! thy guiding spark is fled,
And lasting wretchedness awaits thy bed —
Thy bed of straw! for mark, where even now
O'er their lost child afflicted parents bow ;
Their woe she knows not, but perversely coy,
 Inverted customs yield her sullen joy!
Her midnight meals in secrecy she takes,
Low muttering to the moon, that rising breaks
Through night's dark gloom : — O, how much
    more forlorn
Her night, that knows of no returning
    morn ! —
Slow from the threshold, once her infant seat,
O'er the cold earth she crawls to her retreat ;
Quitting the cot's warm walls, unhoused to
    lie,
Or share the swine's impure and narrow sty ;
The damp night-air her shivering limbs
    assails :
In dreams she moans, and fancied wrongs
    bewails.

When morning wakes, none earlier roused
    than she,
When pendent drops fall glittering from the
    tree.
But naught her rayless melancholy cheers,
Or soothes her breast, or stops her streaming
    tears.
Her matted locks unornamented flow ;
Clasping her knees, and waving to and fro ;—
Her head bowed down, her faded cheek to
    hide ; —
A piteous mourner by the pathway side.
Some tufted molehill through the livelong
    day
She calls her throne : there weeps her life
    away :
And oft the gayly passing stranger stays
His well-timed step, and takes a silent gazes
Till sympathetic drops unbidden start,
And pangs quick springing muster round his
    heart ;
And soft he treads with other gazers round,
And fain would catch her sorrow's plaintive
    sound.
One word alone is all that strikes the ear,

One short, pathetic, simple word, — " O
    dear ! "
A thousand times repeated to the wind,
That wafts the sigh, but leaves the pang be-
    hind !
Forever of the proffered parley shy,
She hears the unwelcome foot advancing nigh;
Nor quite unconscious of her wretched plight,
Gives one sad look and hurries out of sight.

    Fair promised sunbeams of terrestrial bliss,
Health's gallant hopes, — and are ye sunk to
    this ?
For in life's road, though thorns abundant
    grow,
There still are joys poor Poll can never know ;
Joys which the gay companions of her prime
Sip as they drift along the stream of time :
At eve to hear beside their tranquil home
The lifted latch, that speaks the lover come :
That love matured, next playful on the knee
To press the velvet lip of infancy ;
To stay the tottering step, the features
    trace ; —
Inestimable sweets of social peace !

O Thou who bidd'st the vernal juices rise!
Thou, on whose blasts autumnal foliage flies!
Let peace ne'er leave me, nor my heart grow
    cold,
Whilst life and sanity are mine to hold.

  Shorn of their flowers that shed the un-
    treasured seed,
The withering pasture, and the fading mead,
Less tempting grown, diminish more and
    more,
The dairy's pride ; sweet Summer's flowing
    store.
New cares succeed, and gentle duties press,
Where the fireside, a school of tenderness,
Revives the languid chirp, and warms the
    blood
Of cold-nipped weaklings of the latter brood,
That from the shell just bursting into day,
Through yard or pond pursue their venturous
    way.

  Far weightier cares and wider scenes ex-
    pand ;
What devastation marks the new-sown land !

"From hungry woodland's foes go, Giles,
      and guard
The rising wheat, insure its great reward :
A future sustenance, a Summer's pride,
Demand thy vigilance : then be it tried :
Exert thy voice, and wield thy shotless gun :
Go, tarry there from morn till setting sun."

   Keen blows the blast, or ceaseless rain
      descends ;
The half-stripped hedge a sorry shelter lends.
O, for a hovel, e'er so small or low,
Whose roof, repelling winds and early snow,
Might bring home's comforts fresh before
      his eyes !
No sooner thought, than see the structure
      rise,
In some sequestered nook, embanked around,
Sods for its walls, and straw in burdens
      bound !
Dried fuel hoarded is his richest store,
And circling smoke obscures his little door :
Whence creeping forth, to duty's call he
      yields,
And strolls the Crusoe of the lonely fields.

On whitethorns towering, and the leafless rose,
A frost-nipt feast in bright vermilion glows ;
Where clustering sloes in glossy order rise,
He crops the loaded branch ; a cumbrous
    prize :
And o'er the flame the spluttering fruit he
    rests,
Placing green sods to seat the coming
    guests ;
His guests by promise ; playmates young
    and gay : —
But ah ! fresh pastimes lure their steps away !
He sweeps his hearth, and homeward looks
    in vain,
Till feeling disappointment's cruel pain,
His fairy revels are exchanged for rage,
His banquet marred, grown dull his hermit-
    age.
The field becomes his prison, till on high
Benighted birds to shades and coverts fly.
Midst air, health, daylight, can he prisoner
    be ?
If fields are prisons, where is Liberty ?
Here still she dwells, and here her votaries
    stroll ;

But disappointed hope untunes the soul :
Restraints unfelt whilst hours of rapture
    flow,
When troubles press, to chains and barriers
    grow.
Look then from trivial up to greater woes ;
From the poor bird-boy with his roasted sloes,
To where the dungeoned mourner heaves the
    sigh,
Where not one cheering sunbeam meets his
    eye.
Though ineffectual pity thine may be,
No wealth, no power, to set the captive free ;
Though only to thy ravished sight is given
The radiant path that Howard trod to heaven ;
Thy slights can make the wretched more for-
    lorn,
And deeper drive affliction's barbéd thorn.
Say not, "I'll come and cheer thy gloomy
    cell
With news of dearest friends ; how good,
    how well :
I'll be a joyful herald to thine heart " ;
Then fail, and play the worthless trifler's part,
To sip flat pleasures from thy glass's brim,

And waste the precious hour that's due to
    him.
In mercy spare the base, unmanly blow :
Where can he turn, to whom complain of
    you ?
Back to past joys in vain his thoughts may
    stray,
Trace and retrace the beaten, worn out way,
The rankling injury will pierce his breast,
And curses on thee break his midnight rest.

  Bereft of song, and ever-cheering green,
The soft endearments of the Summer scene,
New harmony pervades the solemn wood,
Dear to the soul, and healthful to the blood :
For bold exertion follows on the sound
Of distant sportsmen, and the chiding hound ;
First heard from kennel bursting, mad with
    joy,
Where smiling Euston boasts her good Fitz-
    roy,
Lord of pure alms, and gifts that wide ex-
    tend ;
The farmer's patron, and the poor man's
    friend :

Whose mansion glitters with the eastern ray,
Whose elevated temple points the way,
O'er slopes and lawns, the park's extensive
    pride,
To where the victims of the chase reside,
Ingulfed in earth, in conscious safety warm,
Till lo ! a plot portends their coming harm.

In earliest hours of dark and hooded morn,
Ere yet one rosy cloud bespeaks the dawn,
Whilst far abroad the fox pursues his prey,
He 's doomed to risk the perils of the day,
From his stronghold blocked out ; perhaps to
    bleed,
Or owe his life to fortune or to speed.
For now the pack, impatient rushing on,
Range through the darkest coverts one by one ;
Trace every spot ; whilst down each noble
    glade
That guides the eye beneath a changeful
    shade,
The loitering sportsman feels the instinctive
    flame,
And checks his steed to mark the springing
    game.

Midst intersecting cuts and winding ways
The huntsman cheers his dogs, and anxious
    strays
Where every narrow riding, even shorn,
Gives back the echo of his mellow horn :
Till fresh and lightsome, every power untried,
The starting fugitive leaps by his side,
His lifted finger to his ear he plies,
And the view-halloo bids a chorus rise
Of dogs quick-mouthed, and shouts that min-
    gle loud
As bursting thunder rolls from cloud to cloud.
With ears erect, and chest of vigorous mould,
O'er ditch, o'er fence, unconquerably bold,
The shining courser lengthens every bound,
And his strong footlocks suck the moistened
    ground,
As from the confines of the wood they pour,
And joyous villages partake the roar.
O'er heath far-stretched, or down, or valley
    low,
The stiff-limbed peasant, glorying in the show,
Pursues in vain ; where youth itself soon
    tires,
Spite of the transports that the chase inspires ;

For who unmounted long can charm the eye,
Or hear the music of the leading cry ?

Poor faithful Trouncer ! thou canst lead no
    more ;
All thy fatigues and all thy triumphs o'er !
Triumphs of worth, whose long excelling
    fame
Was still to follow true the hunted game !
Beneath enormous oaks, Britannia's boast,
In thick, impenetrable coverts lost,
When the warm pack in faltering silence
    stood,
Thine was the note that roused the listening
    wood,
Rekindling every joy with tenfold force,
Through all the mazes of the tainted course.
Still foremost thou the dashing stream to
    cross,
And tempt along the animated horse ;
Foremost o'er fen or level mead to pass,
And sweep the showering dew-drops from
    the grass ;
Then bright emerging from the mist below,
To climb the woodland hill's exulting brow.

Pride of thy race! with worth far less than
      thine,
Full many human leaders daily shine!
Less faith, less constancy, less generous
      zeal! —
Then no disgrace my humble verse shall feel,
Where not one lying line to riches bows,
Or poisoned sentiments from rancor flows;
Nor flowers are strewn around Ambition's car:
An honest dog's a nobler theme by far.
Each sportsman heard the tidings with a sigh,
When Death's cold touch had stopt his tune-
      ful cry;
And though high deeds, and fair exalted
      praise,
In memory lived, and flowed in rustic lays,
Short was the strain of monumental woe:
" *Foxes, rejoice! here buried lies your foe.*"
In safety housed, throughout Night's length-
      ening reign,
The cock sends forth a loud and piercing
      strain;
More frequent, as the glooms of midnight flee,
And hours roll round, that brought him lib-
      erty,

When Summer's early dawn, mild, clear, and
    bright,
Chased quick away the transitory night : —
Hours now in darkness veiled ; yet loud the
    scream
Of geese impatient for the playful stream ;
And all the feathered tribe imprisoned raise
Their morning notes of inharmonious praise ;
And many a clamorous hen and cock'rel gay,
When daylight slowly through the fog breaks
    way,
Fly wantonly abroad : but, ah, how soon
The shades of twilight follow hazy noon,
Shortening the busy day ! — day that slides by
Amidst the unfinished toils of husbandry :
Toils still each morn resumed with double
    care
To meet the icy terrors of the year ;
To meet the threats of Boreas undismayed,
And Winter's gathering frowns and hoary head.

    Then welcome, Cold ; welcome, ye snowy
        nights !
Heaven midst your rage shall mingle pure
    delights,

And confidence of hope the soul sustain,
While devastation sweeps along the plain :
Nor shall the child of poverty despair,
But bless the Power that rules the changing
    year ;
Assured — though horrors round his cottage
    reign —
That Spring will come, and Nature smile
    again.

WINTER.

ITH kindred pleasures moved, and
      cares opprest,
  Sharing alike our weariness and rest;
Who lives the daily partner of our hours,
Through every change of heat, and frost, and
    showers,
Partakes our cheerful meals, partaking first
In mutual labor, and fatigue, and thirst;
The kindly intercourse will ever prove
A bond of amity and social love.

To more than man this generous warmth ex-
tends,
And oft the team and shivering herd be-
friends ;
Tender solicitude the bosom fills,
And pity executes what reason wills :
Youth learns compassion's tale from every
tongue,
And flies to aid the helpless and the young.

When now, unsparing as the scourge of war,
Blasts follow blasts, and groves dismantled
roar,
Around their home the storm-pinched cattle
lows,
No nourishment in frozen pastures grows ;
Yet frozen pastures every morn resound
With fair abundance thundering to the
ground.
For though on hoary twigs no buds peep out,
And e'en the hardy brambles cease to sprout,
Beneath dread Winter's level sheets of snow
The sweet nutritious turnip deigns to grow.
Till now imperious Want and wide-spread
Dearth

Bid Labor claim her treasures from the earth.
On Giles, and such as Giles, the labor falls,
To strew the frequent load where hunger
    calls.
On driving gales sharp hail indignant flies,
And sleet, more irksome still, assails his eyes ;
Snow clogs his feet ; or if no snow is seen,
The field with all its juicy store to screen,
Deep goes the frost, till every root is found
A rolling mass of ice upon the ground.
No tender ewe can break her nightly fast,
Nor heifer strong begin the cold repast,
Till Giles with ponderous beetle foremost go,
And scattering splinters fly at every blow ;
When pressing round him, eager for the prize,
From their mixed breath warm exhalations
    rise.

In beaded rows if drops now deck the spray,
While the sun grants a momentary ray,
Let but a cloud's broad shadow intervene,
And stiffened into gems the drops are seen ;
And down the furrowed oak's broad southern
    side
Streams of dissolving rime no longer glide.

Though night approaching bids for rest
    prepare,
Still the flail echoes through the frosty air,
Nor stops till deepest shades of darkness come,
Sending at length the weary laborer home.
From him, with bed and nightly food sup-
    plied,
Throughout the yard, housed round on every
    side,
Deep-plunging cows their rustling feast enjoy,
And snatch sweet mouthfuls from the passing
    boy,
Who moves unseen beneath his trailing load,
Fills the tall racks, and leaves a scattered road ;
Where oft the swine from ambush warm and
    dry
Bolt out, and scamper headlong to their sty,
When Giles with well-known voice, already
    there,
Deigns them a portion of his evening care.

Him, though the cold may pierce, and
    storms molest,
Succeeding hours shall cheer with warmth
    and rest ;

Gladness to spread, and raise the grateful
    smile,
He hurls the fagot bursting from the pile,
And many a log and rifted trunk conveys,
To heap the fire, and wide extend the blaze,
That quivering strong through every opening
    flies,
Whilst smoky columns unobstructed rise.
For the rude architect, unknown to fame
(Nor symmetry nor elegance his aim),
Who spread his floors of solid oak on high,
On beams rough hewn, from age to age that lie,
Bade his wide fabric unimpaired sustain
The orchard's store, and cheese, and golden
    grain ;
Bade from its central base, capacious laid,
The well-wrought chimney rear its lofty
    head ;
Where since hath many a savory ham been
    stored,
And tempests howled and Christmas gambols
    roared.

Flat on the hearth the glowing embers lie,
And flames reflected dance in every eye ;

There the long billet, forced at last to bend,
While gushing sap froths out at either end,
Throws round its welcome heat : — the
    ploughman smiles,
And oft the joke runs hard on sheepish Giles,
Who sits joint tenant of the corner-stool,
The converse sharing, though in duty's school ;
For now attentively 't is his to hear
Interrogations from the master's chair.

    " Left ye your bleating charge, when day-
        light fled,
Near where the haystack lifts its snowy
    head ?
Whose fence of bushy furze, so close and
    warm,
May stop the slanting bullets of the storm.
For, hark ! it blows ; a dark and dismal
    night :
Heaven guide the traveller's fearful steps
    aright !
Now from the woods, mistrustful, and sharp-
    eyed,
The fox in silent darkness seems to glide,
Stealing around us, listening as he goes,

If chance the cock or stammering capon crows,
Or goose, or nodding duck, should darkling
    cry,
As if apprised of lurking danger nigh :
Destruction waits them, Giles, if e'er you
    fail
To bolt their doors against the driving gale.
Strewed you (still mindful of the unsheltered
    head)
Burdens of straw, the cattle's welcome bed ?
Thine heart should feel, what thou mayst
    hourly see,
That *duty's basis is humanity.*
Of pain's unsavory cup though thou must
    taste
(The wrath of Winter from the bleak north-
    east),
Thine utmost sufferings in the coldest day
A period terminates, and joys repay.
Perhaps e'en now, while here those joys we
    boast,
Full many a bark rides down the neighboring
    coast,
Where the high northern waves tremendous
    roar,

Drove down by blasts from Norway's icy
    shore.
The sea-boy there, less fortunate than thou,
Feels all thy pains in all the gusts that blow ;
His freezing hands now drenched, now dry,
    by turns ;
Now lost, now seen, the distant light that
    burns,
On some tall cliff upraised, a flaming guide,
That throws its friendly radiance o'er the tide.
His labors cease not with declining day,
But toils and perils mark his watery way ;
And whilst in peaceful dreams secure we lie,
The ruthless whirlwinds rage along the sky,
Round his head whistling ; — and shalt thou
    repine,
While this protecting roof still shelters
    thine ? "

Mild as the vernal shower, his words pre-
    vail,
And aid the moral precept of his tale :
His wondering hearers learn, and ever keep
These first ideas of the restless deep :
And, as the opening mind a circuit tries,

Present felicities in value rise.
Increasing pleasures every hour they find,
The warmth more precious, and the shelter
  kind ;
Warmth that long reigning bids the eyelids
  close,
As through the blood its balmy influence
  goes,
When the cheered heart forgets fatigues and
  cares,
And drowsiness alone dominion bears.

Sweet then the ploughman's slumbers, hale
  and young,
When the last topic dies upon his tongue ;
Sweet then the bliss his transient dreams in-
  spire,
Till chilblains wake him, or the snapping
  fire :
He starts, and ever thoughtful of his team,
Along the glittering snow a feeble gleam
Shoots from his lantern, as he yawning goes
To add fresh comforts to their night's repose ;
Diffusing fragrance as their food he moves,
And pats the jolly sides of those he loves.

Thus full replenished, perfect ease possest,
From night till morn alternate food and rest,
No rightful cheer withheld, no sleep debarred,
Their each day's labor brings its sure reward.
Yet when from plough or lumbering cart set
        free,
They taste awhile the sweets of liberty :
E'en sober Dobbin lifts his clumsy heel
And kicks, disdainful of the dirty wheel ;
But soon, his frolic ended, yields again
To trudge the road, and wear the clinking
        chain.

    Short-sighted Dobbin! — thou canst only
        see
The trivial hardships that encompass thee :
Thy chains were freedom, and thy toils re-
        pose,
Could the poor post-horse tell thee all his
        woes,
Show thee his bleeding shoulders, and unfold
The dreadful anguish he endures for gold :
Hired at each call of business, lust, or rage,
That prompts the traveller on from stage to
        stage.

Still on his strength depends their boasted
    speed ;
For them his limbs grow weak, his bare ribs
    bleed ;
And though he groaning quickens at com-
    mand,
Their extra shilling in the rider's hand
Becomes his bitter scourge, — 't is he must feel
The double efforts of the lash and steel ;
Till when, up hill, the destined hill he gains,
And, trembling under complicated pains,
Prone from his nostrils, darting on the
    ground,
His breath emitted floats in clouds around ;
Drops chase each other down his chest and
    sides,
And spattered mud his native color hides :
Through his swoln veins the boiling torrent
    flows,
And every nerve a separate torture knows.
His harness loosed, he welcomes, eager-eyed,
The pail's full draught that quivers by his
    side ;
And joys to see the well-known stable-door,
As the starved mariner the friendly shore.

Ah, well for him if here his suffering ceased,
And ample hours of rest his pains appeased !
But roused again, and sternly bade to rise,
And shake refreshing slumber from his eyes,
Ere his exhausted spirits can return,
Or through his frame reviving ardor burn,
Come forth he must, though limping, maimed,
    and sore ;
He hears the whip, the chaise is at the
    door : —
The collar tightens, and again he feels
His half-healed wounds inflamed; again the
    wheels
With tiresome sameness in his ears resound,
O'er blinding dust, or miles of flinty ground.
Thus nightly robbed and injured day by
    day,
His peacemeal murderers wear his life away.
What sayest thou, Dobbin ? what though
    hounds await
With open jaws the moment of thy fate,
No better fate attends his public race ;
His life is misery, and his end disgrace.
Then freely bear thy burden to the mill ;
Obey but one short law, — thy driver's will.

Affection, to thy memory ever true,
Shall boast of mighty loads that Dobbin
    drew ;
And back to childhood shall the mind with
    pride
Recount thy gentleness in many a ride
To pond, or field, or village fair, when thou
Held'st high thy braided main and comely
    brow ;
And oft the tale shall rise to homely fame
Upon thy generous spirit and thy name.

    Though faithful to a proverb we regard
The midnight chieftain of the farmer's yard,
Beneath whose guardianship all hearts re-
  •   joice,
Woke by the echo of his hollow voice ;
Yet as the hound may faltering quit the pack,
Snuff the foul scent and hasten yelping back :
And e'en the docile pointer know disgrace,
Thwarting the general instinct of his race ;
E'en so the mastiff, or the meaner cur,
At times will from the path of duty err
(A pattern of fidelity by day,
By night a murderer, lurking for his prey),

And round the pastures or the fold will creep,
And, coward-like, attack the peaceful sheep.
Alone the wanton mischief he pursues,
Alone in reeking blood his jaws imbrues ;
Chasing amain his frightened victims round,
Till death in wild confusion strews the
      ground ;
Then wearied out, to kennel sneaks away,
And licks his guilty paws till break of day.

The deed discovered, and the news once
      spread,
Vengeance hangs o'er the unknown culprit's
      head :
And careful shepherds extra hours bestow
In patient watchings for the common foe, —
A foe most dreaded now, when rest and peace
Should wait the season of the flock's increase.

In part these nightly terrors to dispel,
Giles, ere he sleeps, his little flock must tell.
From the fireside with many a shrug he hies,
Glad if the full-orbed moon salute his eyes,
And through the unbroken stillness of the
      night

Shed on his path her beams of cheering light.
With sauntering step he climbs the distant
    stile,
Whilst all around him wears a placid smile ;
There views the white-robed clouds in clus-
    ters driven,
And all the glorious pageantry of heaven.
Low, on the utmost boundary of the sight,
The rising vapors catch the silver light ;
Thence Fancy measures, as they parting fly,
Which first will throw its shadow on the eye,
Passing the source of light, and thence away,
Succeeded quick by brighter still than they.
Far yet above these wafted clouds are seen
(In a remoter sky, still more serene)
Others, detached in ranges through the air,
Spotless as snow, and countless as they 're fair ;
Scattered immensely wide from east to west,
The beauteous semblance of a flock at rest.
These, to the raptured mind, aloud proclaim
Their Mighty Shepherd's everlasting name.

Whilst thus the loiterer's utmost stretch of
    soul
Climbs the still clouds, or passes those that roll,

And loosed imagination soaring goes
High o'er his home, and all his little woes,
Time glides away ; neglected duty calls ;
At once from plains of light to earth he falls,
And down a narrow lane, well known by day,
With all his speed pursues his sounding way,
In thought still half absorbed and chilled with
      cold,
When lo ! an object frightful to behold ;
A grisly spectre, clothed in silver-gray,
Around whose feet the waving shadows play,
Stands in his path ! — He stops, and not a
      breath
Heaves from his heart, that sinks almost to
      death.
Loud the owl halloos o'er his head unseen ;
All else is silent, dismally serene :
Some prompt ejaculation, whispered low,
Yet bears him up against the threatening foe ;
And thus poor Giles, though half inclined to
      fly,
Mutters his doubts, and strains his steadfast
      eye.
" 'T is not my crimes thou com'st here to re-
      prove ;

No murders stain my soul, no perjured love ;
If thou 'rt indeed what here thou seem'st to
    be,
Thy dreadful mission cannot reach to me.
By parents taught still to mistrust mine eyes,
Still to approach each object of surprise,
Lest Fancy's formful visions should deceive
In moonlight paths, or glooms of falling eve,
This then 's the moment when my mind should
    try
To scan thy motionless deformity ;
But O, the fearful task ! yet well I know
An aged ash, with many a spreading bough
(Beneath whose leaves I 've found a Summer's
    bower,
Beneath whose trunk I 've weathered many a
    shower),
Stands singly down this solitary way,
But far beyond where now my footsteps stay.
'T is true, thus far I 've come with heedless
    haste ;
No reckoning kept, no passing objects traced.
And can I then have reached that very tree ?
Or is its reverend form assumed by thee ?"
The happy thought alleviates his pain :

He creeps another step ; then stops again ;
Till slowly, as his noiseless feet draw near,
Its perfect lineaments at once appear ;
Its crown of shivering ivy whispering peace,
And its white bark that fronts the moon's pale
        face.
Now, whilst his blood mounts upward, now
        he knows
The solid gain that from conviction flows ;
And strengthened confidence shall hence fulfil
(With conscious innocence more valued still)
The dreariest task that Winter nights can
        bring,
By churchyard dark, or grove, or fairy ring ;
Still buoying up the timid mind of youth,
Till loitering Reason hoists the scale of Truth.
With these blest guardians Giles his course
        pursues,
Till, numbering his heavy-sided ewes,
Surrounding stillness tranquillize his breast,
And shape the dreams that wait his hours of
        rest.

    As when retreating tempests we behold,
Whose skirts at length the azure sky unfold,

And full of murmurings and mingled wrath,
Siowly unshroud the smiling face of earth,
Bringing the bosom joy : so Winter flies ! —
And see the source of life and light uprise!
A heightening arch o'er southern hills he
        bends,
Warm on the cheek the slanting beam descends,
And gives the reeking mead a brighter hue,
And draws the modest primrose-bud to view.
Yet frosts succeed, and winds impetuous rush,
And hail-storms rattle through the budding
        bush ;
And night-fallen lambs require the shepherd's
        care,
And teeming ewes, that still their burdens
        bear ;
Beneath whose sides to-morrow's dawn may
        see
The milk-white strangers bow the trembling
        knee ;
At whose first birth the powerful instinct's
        seen
That fills with champions the daisied green :
For ewes that stood aloof with fearful eye,
With stamping foot now men and dogs defy,

And, obstinately faithful to their young,
Guard their first steps to join the bleating
    throng.

  But casualties and death from damps and
    cold
Will still attend the well-conducted fold :
Her tender offspring dead, the dam aloud
Calls, and runs wild amidst the unconscious
    crowd :
And orphaned sucklings raise the piteous cry ;
No wool to warm them, no defenders nigh.
And must her streaming milk then flow in
    vain ?
Must unregarded innocence complain ?
No ; — ere this strong solicitude subside,
Maternal fondness may be fresh applied,
And the adopted stripling still may find
A parent most assiduously kind.
For this he 's doomed a while disguised to
    range
(For fraud or force must work the wished-for
    change) ;
For this his predecessor's skin he wears,
Till, cheated into tenderness and cares,

The unsuspecting dam, contented grown,
Cherish and guard the fondlings as her own.

Thus all by turns to fair perfection rise ;
Thus twins are parted to increase their size :
Thus instinct yields as interest points the way,
Till the bright flock, augmenting every day,
On sunny hills and vales of springing flowers
With ceaseless clamor greet the vernal hours.

The humbler shepherd here with joy be-
        holds
The approved economy of crowded folds,
And, in his small contracted round of cares,
Adjusts the practice of each hint he hears ;
For boys with emulation learn to glow,
And boast their pastures, and their healthful
        show
Of well-grown lambs, the glory of the Spring ;
And field to field in competition bring.
E'en Giles, for all his cares and watchings
        past,
And all his contests with the wintry blast,
Claims a full share of that sweet praise be-
        stowed

By gazing neighbors, when along the road,
Or village green, his curly coated throng
Suspends the chorus of the spinner's song ;
When admiration's unaffected grace
Lisps from the tongue, and beams in every
    face :
Delightful moments ! — sunshine, health, and
    joy
Play round, and cheer the elevated boy !
" Another Spring ! " his heart exulting cries ;
" Another year !" with promised blessings
    rise ! —
" Eternal Power ! from whom those blessings
    flow,
Teach me still more to wonder, more to know:
Seed-time and harvest let me see again ;
Wander the leaf-strewn wood, the frozen
    plain :
Let the first flower, corn-waving field, plain,
    tree,
Here round my home still lift my soul to
    thee ;
And let me ever, midst thy bounties, raise
An humble note of thankfulness and praise !"